"What are you doing, showing up naked in my bed, lass?"

Her fantasy man's voice was even deeper and richer than she'd imagined, with a thick Scottish burr. Under normal circumstances, she'd find the voice, along with the rest of him, very sexy...but there was nothing normal about this situation.

Kate scrambled for something to cover herself. "Hand me that scarf, will you?"

"Scarf?"

She pointed to the long plaid scarf he held in his hands. The one that matched his kilt. "Yeah, you know? Your scarf."

"Are you daft, woman, that you'd call me plaid a scarf? But if that is what it takes..." Without further ado, he unwound the remaining length of material and tossed it to her.

Oh. My. God. The bottom and top were one piece of cloth, and he was totally bare beneath it. She saw naked bodies all the time, but this was different. *Very* different. She swallowed hard and tried to drag her eyes back up to his face. "You could have told me you weren't wearing anything beneath it."

His smile held a wealth of masculine arrogance. "But lass, *you didna ask....*"

Dear Reader,

When I first heard about a time-travel miniseries in Harlequin Blaze™ I knew I wanted to write one. Correction—I *had* to write one.

I love reading historicals, especially Scottish historicals. *Braveheart* and *Rob Roy* are two of my favorite movies. What time period did I want? Who was my hero? My response was instinctual—a Highland chieftain. Darach MacTavish is not only his own man, but very much a product of his time. While I aimed for historical accuracy regarding the political/social climate before and after the Battle of Culloden, I took creative license with the rest. The clans MacTavish and Campbell are real, but in no way does this story reflect their history. And to all you Campbells, those portrayed in this story were merely a rogue lot.

It is said that a writer imbues every book with a bit of themselves. I'm not an E.R. physician, but I very much relate to Kate Wexford. She's a twenty-first-century woman who enjoys all the conveniences of her time: the advances of modern medicine, electricity, cell phones, the Internet, flush toilets, debit cards, the right to own property—you get the idea.

This book proved to be an incredible writing experience. What began as a fun little time travel became a story of soul mates who discover a love so powerful it transcends time. I hope you enjoy Kate and Darach's love story and their journey through time. I would love to hear from you. Drop by to visit me at my Web site, www.jenniferlabrecque.com, e-mail me at Jennifer@jenniferlabrecque.com, or write me via snail mail at P.O. Box 298, Hiram, GA 30141.

Enjoy,

Jennifer LaBrecque

HIGHLAND FLING
Jennifer LaBrecque

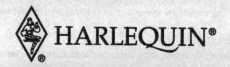

TORONTO • NEW YORK • LONDON
AMSTERDAM • PARIS • SYDNEY • HAMBURG
STOCKHOLM • ATHENS • TOKYO • MILAN • MADRID
PRAGUE • WARSAW • BUDAPEST • AUCKLAND

ISBN-13: 978-0-373-79266-5
ISBN-10:   0-373-79266-2

HIGHLAND FLING

This edition published by arrangement with Harlequin Books S.A.

www.eHarlequin.com

Printed in U.S.A.

ABOUT THE AUTHOR

Jennifer LaBrecque writes contemporary romantic fiction—or at least she did, until she decided to try her hand at a time travel and got hooked! Still, while she enjoyed the experience, she likes writing for Harlequin Blaze—*usually* a very contemporary series—more. Jennifer lives in suburban Atlanta with one husband, one daughter, two cats, two greyhounds and a Chihuahua who runs the whole show.

Books by Jennifer LaBrecque

HARLEQUIN BLAZE
206—DARING IN THE DARK
228—ANTICIPATION

HARLEQUIN TEMPTATION
886—BARELY MISTAKEN
904—BARELY DECENT
952—BARELY BEHAVING
992—BETTER THAN CHOCOLATE
1012—REALLY HOT!

Don't miss any of our special offers. Write to us at the following address for information on our newest releases.

Harlequin Reader Service
U.S.: 3010 Walden Ave., P.O. Box 1325, Buffalo, NY 14269
Canadian: P.O. Box 609, Fort Erie, Ont. L2A 5X3

To Dr. David K. Monson, surgeon extraordinaire.
Thank you for "rescuing" my leg
and giving it a happy ever after.
You're my hero.

1

KATE TRACED THE PUCKERED, rough edge of the scar that ran from his side across the smooth satin of his back. He was warm and—

"Dr. Wexford, could you take a look at Mr. Chesney's x-ray before you leave?"

—he was a figment of her imagination. The intern's question jerked her back to the present. It was a good thing her shift was ending, if she was daydreaming by the coffee machine again. She was officially off-duty, but she could spare the time to check an x-ray. Not only did she love what she did, it was off-duty dedication that had earned her the position of assistant head of ER at Atlanta's prestigious Walker Medical Center.

"Absolutely." Kate drained the rest of her double latte with the espresso shot, took the film and held it up to the fluorescent light. She shook her head. Work in a city ER was neither boring nor predictable. "Did Mr. Chesney give you any indication he has a small rodent in his rectal area?"

Dave Reddick, straight out of med school, nearly choked. "No, doctor, he didn't."

"My guess is a female hamster, three to four months old. I think Dyer's on the surgical rotation. See when he wants to schedule Mr. Chesney to retrieve his friend."

Kate handed the x-ray back to the fresh-faced Reddick and headed for the door.

"Uh, Dr. Wexford?"

She stopped and turned. "Yes?"

"How'd you know?"

"The pointy nose and long tail was a dead give-away."

"Uh, no ma'am. I meant how'd you know it was a female, three to four months old?"

"Oh that." Kate shrugged and smiled at the earnest resident. "I made that part up."

Reddick's mouth dropped open and then he recovered and offered a stilted laugh. "Right."

"But he does need to have it surgically removed so get him scheduled." She walked out of the break-room and ducked into the staff bathroom.

Good. It was empty. She checked her watch. Forty-five minutes. She could still make it before the museum closed, even though she'd sworn she wasn't going back again. She shrugged out of her white coat and hung it in the locker, knowing it was inevitable.

Tonight was the last night. After tonight it was a moot point. But all day she'd felt this odd compulsion, almost, as silly as it sounded, a calling to see him one more time. No. It was beyond silly. Kate had always prided herself on her practical, pragmatic nature. She didn't do things like show up again and again to moon over a man in a portrait. But tonight was the last night. What harm could come of one more foolish trip?

She dragged a brush through her short hair. Hmm. Time to schedule a touch-up. She had major root action going on. She dug around in her purse and pulled out her lipstick.

The door behind her opened and two women strolled in. Oh, great. Dr. Torri Campbell, the Bitch from Hell and her underling who reminded Kate of Nurse Ratchett.

Kate ignored the two women and leaned into the mirror to smooth on her lipstick.

"Hot date tonight, Dr. Wexford?" Torri arched one perfect blond brow, her green catlike eyes alight with malice.

Kate and Torri had pulled ER rotations at the same hospital out of med school and then later found themselves at Walker Medical Center vying for the same position. They'd never particularly hit it off, but once Kate had been named assistant head of ER, Torri had all but declared war.

"Yes, I do have a hot date waiting, Dr. Campbell. Thanks for asking."

Torri, a tall statuesque blonde who used a Palm Pilot to juggle her numerous dates and men, knew good and well Kate Wexford didn't have a date. Why break a six-month dry spell?

"New man in your life? How in the world did I miss that?" If a person could expire from sheer bitchiness, Torri would've been six feet under long ago.

Kate, her wicked sense of humor fully engaged, decided in for a penny, in for a pound. She imbued her shrug with just the right amount of insouciance to pique the other woman's curiosity. "Just someone who's been in town a few weeks. He travels often and he's leaving again tomorrow." The truth was getting more and more elastic, but the stretch was worth the look on Torri's perfect features.

"Ooh." Torri slanted her a look rife with speculation. "Where's he from?"

"He's a world traveler, but he's originally from Scotland." Okay, so there was a good chance she'd burn in hell for this, but it was just too much fun.

"Well, aren't you the secretive one. How'd you meet him?"

"A mutual friend introduced us."

"Blind date?" Torri eyed Kate, who was fully two

inches shorter and twenty pounds heavier, as if the guy would have to be blind to continue going out with her. At least Kate didn't target married men. She'd spotted Torri and one very married surgeon lip-locking in the parking garage last week. Not that she was in the market for either, but Kate would take a blind date over a married man any day.

"Something like that." She shrugged into her coat. It was ridiculous that one look could negate all her achievements and reduce her once again to the short, overweight girl who'd made the grades but not the social calendar. "Got to run. I don't want to keep him waiting." She slung her purse over one shoulder and headed toward the door.

"Hold on." Torri reached into her locker, pulled out a handful of condoms and stuffed them into Kate's purse. "Friends don't let friends head into the weekend unprotected."

She and her underling exchanged a glance that clearly stated Torri was hot, Kate was not and that she'd need a handful of condoms was a stretch. An even bigger stretch was that she and Torri were friends.

"Thanks." Kate opened the door.

"Sure. Don't do anything I wouldn't." Torri offered a brittle laugh. "And that leaves it wide open."

Maybe it was the end of a grueling twelve-hour shift, maybe it was the caffeine surge from the espresso, or maybe it was because she was no longer a sixteen year old wallflower suffering from the digs the "popular" girls had thrown at her, but she gave in to the impulse she'd squelched more than once.

"Thanks, but I think I'll stick with unmarried men." She smiled and let the door close behind her.

God that felt good. She bypassed the parking garage. Friday rush hour was still alive and near gridlock even at this late hour. Atlanta was a great city, but the traffic was abysmal. She could hoof it or forget about making it there before it closed.

She was only slightly winded twenty minutes later when she mounted the leaf-strewn marble steps and flashed her membership card at the blazer-clad attendant.

"You know we close in fifteen minutes," she said.

"Yes. Thanks."

She hurried along the winding, stairless ramp that lead to the different levels of the museum, too impatient to wait on the ridiculously slow elevator. Besides, she could use the exercise. With its switch-back ramp, the building reminded her of a giant chambered nautilus.

Her heart thudded and it was more than the

exertion of the climb. She felt as nervous as if she were meeting a real date.

Here it was. Third floor, one left turn and she was at the special traveling exhibit, Sex through the Ages. Virtually deserted. Only one couple, holding hands and talking in low tones, wandered in the opposite direction.

Excitement hummed through her like a low current of energy. It had been this way since the first time she'd stepped into the room a month ago. It had been a Friday night, much like this evening, but instead of closing in fifteen minutes, the museum had been open late. It had been one of the Friday Evenings of Jazz the museum hosted to launch a new exhibit. A jazz quartet had played in the open rotunda and a cash bar served martinis.

Half a martini into the evening, she'd wandered through the display of dildos throughout history and another display covering the transition of tempting undergarments through the ages. Kate wasn't sure the thong counted as real progress.

She'd just wandered out of that room and into another, not certain of the theme there, a saxophone's husky notes floating through the night air around her. And that's when she'd first felt it. A raw sexual energy had pulsed deep inside, a need that blossomed in her womb and radiated through her.

The scent of a man, unfettered by any of the myriad male colognes on the market, but with just a hint of something indefinable, had teased her nose and a purely instinctual response had quivered through her. She'd felt his breath feather over her skin, felt his heat near her, felt his lust and his hunger.

She'd never felt such energy from anyone else. And never been quite so aroused without a look or a touch.

She'd turned, fully expecting to find a man right behind her. There'd been no one. Instead, there'd only been a painting. *The* painting. Mounted on the wall behind her.

She'd felt the same energy, an answering hum deep within her every time she'd visited the exhibit, which had been often. It was crazy. She wasn't just a woman in charge of her own life, she was the assistant head of one of the busiest ER's in the city. But it was as if her will had been sublimated and she couldn't resist coming—even when she tried to stay away.

And it was the same now as it had been then, when she'd first seen him.

"Now that's a man," Kate Wexford sighed at the rendering of the rugged Scotsman towering over the ancient bed. A wicked scar, the one she'd day-dreamed of earlier, bisected the sleek muscles in his bare back. With arms like small saplings, he eased his kilt, a red and blue plaid, down his hips, one knee braced on the bed's platform, his legs thick and strong. Wild hair as dark as a starless night curled past the width of his massive shoulders. Not for the first time, she speculated that all parts were probably equally large.

In the background of the picture, a fire burned in the stone wall, burnishing his body with a golden glow, casting the woman on the bed in shadow, only her foot visible.

Kate berated herself for the heat that flooded her. What was wrong with her that she had the hots for a freaking picture? But it had beckoned her and brought her back with growing frequency. The man in the picture had increasingly intruded on her thoughts and even interrupted her focus at work. Kate knew she could be single-minded and determined, but she'd never been obsessive. But, clearly, that had changed with this picture, this man.

But not after tonight. The exhibit ended today. Tomorrow it would travel to another city. Irrationally, a deep mourning of bidding a lover farewell gripped her. Heat and yearning and no small measure of resentment flowed through her. She was being ridiculous and even more pathetic than Torri Campbell made her out to be—lusting after some dead guy in a painting who most likely had never been a real person anyway. And logical, sensible Kate didn't do ridiculous or romantic.

That was more in keeping with her former college roomie, Jordan. Jordan, now back in grad school, lost herself for days in times long past and ancient cultures.

"It seems you've taken a liking to the MacTavish," a voice behind her said.

Kate started and turned, annoyed at the interruption. She relaxed. It was only the older man she'd seen on several occasions. With his gray hair, kind blue eyes and frayed vest, he reminded her of an old-fashioned conductor who'd collected countless tickets for innumerable journeys. Nonetheless, he'd startled her.

"Excuse me?"

"I'm the exhibit caretaker." He nodded toward the starkly sensual portrait. "You come often. You seem to have taken a liking to the MacTavish."

Busted. And although it was embarrassing the number of times she'd visited this portrait, she could hardly deny it when the old man had clearly noted her obsession.

She flushed at being caught out and nodded. So, her man had a name. Her curiosity outweighed her embarrassment. "Yes, I'm fairly taken with…what did you call him, the MacTavish? So, he's real? Or, I mean, he was?"

The old man studied the portrait as if viewing an old friend. "Darach MacTavish. Once head of the clan MacTavish. One of the finest men to walk Scottish soil."

Kate drew a deep breath, her heart pounding. He was real. Well, he had been real.

"Who painted the picture?" She'd often wondered.

"The artist is unknown."

"Who's the woman in the portrait?" Talk about total irrationality to resent the woman in the picture.

"That's unknown as well. I do know Darach MacTavish died shortly after the picture was painted."

His words knifed through her soul. What was wrong with her? She dealt with life and death on a daily basis and while she wasn't inured, she handled it.

Kate persevered, driven by the knowledge that after tonight this man who'd so captured her imagination would be forever gone from her world. "What happened? How'd he die?"

"The Battle of Culloden."

Kate looked at him blankly. The man in the painting might have captured her imagination and awakened a fierce lust, but she was a doctor, not a historian. Science, not history, had always been her thing. "Never heard of it."

"A group of Scotsmen known as Jacobites wanted to restore Bonnie Prince Charles to the English throne. It was a doomed endeavor from the beginning. Darach MacTavish died on the battlefield at Drumossie Moor, later known as Culloden, in the spring of 1745. Even if he hadn't, the British would've killed him afterwards."

Kate gasped and braced her hand against the wall as a physical pain wracked her body. "What about his wife? His children?"

"No wife. No children. The MacTavish died without any heirs."

"So he died alone." Unbidden, the thought came to her that if she died tonight, now, she too would die alone, much as the man depicted before her. With both of her parents dead and no time for a boy-friend or husband or even girlfriends with her schedule, who would miss her?

The old man shook his head, his eyes looking beyond her and the present, into the past. "He didn't die alone. His clansmen died along with him on that bloody field. Them that didn't die along with him were hunted down by the British. And that was the end of the clan MacTavish." He shook his head. "Actually, that day marked the end of the Highland clans."

It was her turn to shake her head. His story, in

addition to eating up her last few minutes, had irrationally devastated her. "It seems such a waste. But I don't suppose any of us can avoid our destinies." It sounded better than life's a bitch and then you die. This obsession she'd developed couldn't be mentally healthy. It was just as well the exhibit would leave Atlanta after tonight.

The old man's enigmatic smile vaguely unsettled her. "Destiny's an interesting concept. Did you know Albert Einstein was fully convinced time was yet another frontier to be explored?"

"I think I've read that before. But I don't believe it's possible." She started as the lights in the main section of the building dimmed, reducing the room to shadows.

"It's time for you to go, Miss."

Intellectually, she knew her time was up. The logical part of her wanted to turn and leave. The new, unfamiliar part of her awakened by the portrait balked at leaving just yet. "I know the museum's closed, but do you think you could give me another minute?"

His look apologized. "It's time for you to go now. Do you have everything you need?"

His words penetrated her heavy heart with their peculiarity. "Everything I need?"

"Are your affairs in order?"

The old man took her by the arm, but then rather than turning toward the door, he propelled her closer to the picture. She was too surprised to protest or pull away when he gave her a shove. Instead of banging into the wall, she felt herself spinning, faster and faster. Dizzy. Disoriented. Unable to…get…her… bearings. Dark…closing…in….

2

KATE SHOOK HER HEAD to clear it. At least the spinning had stopped. She opened her eyes, and immediately closed them again.

What the hell…?

"Well, lass, mayhap you shoulda asked before you showed up naked in my bed. I wouldn't complain, except you are a stranger. I well nigh ken everyone in these hills."

Her fantasy man's voice was even deeper and richer than she'd imagined with a thick Scottish burr. Under normal circumstances she'd find the voice, along with the rest of him, very sexy…but there was nothing normal about finding yourself naked on a bed with a very large stranger looming over you.

Her brain raced as she opened her eyes and scanned her surroundings. Someone had gone to a lot of trouble to replicate the exact setting of the painting, even down to the fire crackling beyond the stone hearth. She looked for any hidden cameras on the set. She wasn't sure how they'd done it. How had they gotten her out of her clothes? This had to be some over-the-top reality show set or she was an un- witting participant in an elaborate hoax.

Kate possessed a sense of humor. She appreci- ated a good joke, but *naked?* How had they gotten her here? One minute she'd been standing in the museum looking at the picture and talking to the caretaker. The next minute, he shoved her, she blacked out, and came to *in* the picture...and naked as a newborn at that. She was more annoyed than frightened. "This isn't funny. If you don't put an end to this immediately, I might have to sue someone's ass off."

She scrambled for something to cover herself. Her clothes had vanished, but her purse still hung from her shoulder. Regardless of how sexy Tall, Dark and Yummy came across, he needed to know she meant business. She shifted the purse to her front, trying to shield herself.

"And you can cut the accent." She raised her voice and spoke to the room at large, so any hidden microphones could pick her up clearly. "If some- one's rolling tape cut it right now and we'll just forget about a lawsuit."

Despite the affable smile curling his lips, the

man's dark eyes raked her, assessed her. Even under the bizarre circumstances, a betraying heat spread through her.

"And I want my clothes." She used the tone that always got results. "Now."

"Do ye now? I'm perfectly fine with the view. And I have no idea where you left your clothes, lass." He pulled out a short dagger and the first frisson of fear replaced her confusion. "Pass along that satchel you're holding onto and I will check that your clothes are not in there."

Kate clutched her Prada bag even closer. "Forget it. I'm not handing over my purse." She ran an unsteady hand over the bag. No bulge of clothes there, even though she hadn't expected there to be. "My clothes aren't in there. Now, Mr. Whoever You Are, hand over my clothes."

He shrugged massive shoulders that gleamed in the firelight and glanced around the room. "They are nae here. And mayhap you could tell me who you are and how you came to be in my bed without your clothes."

"I'm not discussing anything until I've got something to put on. That scarf of yours is better than nothing." Kate was used to immediate compliance. She absolutely wouldn't let him see that he, along with the whole situation, confused her.

"Scarf?"

Kate pointed to the long plaid scarf he held in his hands. The one that matched his kilt. "Yeah, your scarf."

"Are you daft, woman, that you would call me plaid a scarf? But if that's what it takes to get an answer out of you...." Without further ado he unwound the remaining length of material and tossed it to her.

Oh. My. God. The bottom and the top were all one long piece of material and he was stark naked beneath it. She saw naked bodies all the time, but this was different. Vastly different. She swallowed hard and dragged her eyes back up to his face. No need to gape like a hysterical virgin or a sex-starved spinster.

"You could've told me you didn't have on anything beneath it."

"You didna ask." His smile held a wealth of arrogance.

For an instant, Kate considered tossing the material back at him, but if one of them had to be naked...well, better him than her. Plus, if you had to have a naked man standing by a bed...well, he was a fine specimen.

"Who's in charge here?" she asked as she wrapped the material, still bearing his body heat and his hauntingly familiar scent, around herself toga-style.

He cocked his head to one side and looked down the hooked nose that saved his face from being too pretty. "You're wearing the MacTavish colors and you have to ask?"

This whole thing was way too weird and she might've been more open to the practical joke if she hadn't been naked and if the now-naked man wasn't wielding a knife. "Oh yeah, how could I forget? You're Darach MacTavish…and I'm the Queen of England."

The words were hardly out of her mouth when she found herself pinned flat on her back, the man atop her. The cool metal of his dagger bit against her neck. His eyes were flat and cold. "I'm not sure whether you are daft or bold or both, but those are dangerous words to speak on MacTavish land."

For the first time, Kate was thoroughly frightened, not just because she was being straddled by a knife-wielding naked psycho, but for the first time she recognized this might be something other than a hoax.

Perhaps it was the flicker of fear in her eyes, but the man moved the blade away from her throat.

"Thank you," she gasped, only then realizing she'd been holding her breath, afraid to breathe.

He slid off of her. "I'm sorry to have frightened you."

"I apologize for my earlier sarcasm. Obviously I'm not the Queen of England. I don't even like the royal family and I think it was extremely tacky for Charles to marry that Camilla." She caught herself. Fear had her babbling like the proverbial brook. "My name is Kate Wexford. Dr. Kate Wexford. Where exactly am I?"

Pity, along with a hearty dose of mistrust, warred in his eyes, as if she were the one suffering psychological problems. "Where would you like to be, Kate-lass?"

"Back where I was five minutes ago? Looking at this picture instead of standing in it. Where am I?"

The man stepped back a pace to stand tall and proud by the bedside, dagger still in hand. "You're in the keep of Castle MacTavish at Glenagan."

Truly. Not much escaped her, but she was having a heck of a time keeping up with *this*. She dealt with the regular druggies and the occasional psychotic in the ER. This man didn't have the wild-eyed, high-on-drugs look or the psychotic demeanor, but humoring him seemed the best course of action. "And you're Darach MacTavish?"

He bowed formally from the waist, as if he were garbed in royalty's finest and wasn't splendidly, impressively naked before her. "Aye, I am the Mac-Tavish, laird of Glenagan."

And just how out of touch with reality was he? "And what year is it?"

"The year be 1744." He thought it was 17-freaking-44? Okay. "What year might you think it?" He spoke carefully, as if *she* was the one with the problem. Delusional people were actually more pitiful than frightening, except those armed with knives—that was a bad combination.

She hedged. "Uh…I thought it might be a little later than that." She carefully slid to the edge of the bed. "So, it was nice to meet you Darach MacTavish but I think I should be going now."

"And where might you be heading?" His low, rich voice held a note of indulgence.

"I should really be getting home. I have lots of people who'll worry if I don't get home." And that was one whopping lie and a half. Unfortunately, no one would miss her until she didn't turn up for her next shift two days from now. Even then no one would worry because Torri Campbell would eagerly snitch that Kate was indulging in a condom-a-thon.

"And where are your people?" His raised brows lent him a distinctly wicked, in a pulse-quickening way, look.

Okay. She'd play his game, as if he didn't know from where she'd been abducted. "Atlanta. Atlanta, Georgia."

His brow furrowed as though in confusion.

"It's dark," he said, nodding his head toward the

window cut high into the stone wall, "and night's no place for a lass alone. Rest, Kate, and in the morn we'll return you to your people."

Exhaustion flooded her body and her mind. It was more than she could assimilate. However, she deduced that Darach MacTavish, or whoever was standing naked before her like some warrior of old obviously meant her no harm. That time had come and gone.

"You aren't going to tie me up are you?"

A glimmer of a smile lurked in his eyes and crooked one corner of his sensual mouth. "I can if you want me to, but it's not necessary. You are free to leave, but I wouldna advise it."

"Why not?"

"You are a stranger to these parts. If you leave this room, the women would stone you. The men...well, they aren't adverse to a comely lass, daft or no. I mean you no harm, Kate Wexford. If I did, you'd have already found it. And don't think of trying to take my dagger while I sleep. Men have died for less."

Having felt the press of his blade, she didn't doubt it. She wrapped the soft wool more tightly around her, ensconcing herself in the same scent that had beckoned to her when she'd been drawn to the damn painting in the first place. Had it been only half an hour ago or a lifetime? She glanced at her watch. It had stopped. This situation was getting weirder by the minute.

And despite the fact that she felt leaden with fatigue, there was no way she was sleeping until she got some answers. But she'd pretend to sleep and then when Tall, Dark and Naked drifted off to la-la land, she'd nose around and see what she could find out.

"I'm not interested in your dagger," she said, reassuring him. Unfortunately, with his dagger by his side, it was difficult to look at the blade rather than his private sword.

"Be a good lass and get some rest."

When had anyone last spoken to her in that patronizing tone? Who did he think he was? Oh, yeah. He thought he was the laird of Glenagan. Her eyes drifted closed. She'd…fake…him out until…he…slept….

DARACH KNEW THE MOMENT sleep claimed Kate Wexford. What he still didn't know, however, was what manner of woman she was. Without question, she was different, with her strange accent and speech and her hair shorn in the manner of a lad. And with all of her odd ways, why had he felt a recognition in his soul, as if he knew her? And how the devil had she found her way to his bed?

He watched her sleep, noting the dark smudges beneath her eyes where her lashes fanned over her cheeks, the bow of her upper lip, the roundness of her bare shoulder, the curve of her breasts and hips covered by his plaid, the delicate arch of her bare feet. And he felt something inside, the same thing he'd first felt when he'd seen her on his bed, a tingle that ran through him from toe to finger tip.

Kate Wexford should have been stopped by his guard-at-arms. Barring that, she should have never made it past the grand hall to the keep. Of certain, she never should have gained access to his chamber. Was everyone in his house asleep or simply daft? By all that was holy, Hamish would answer to him.

He crossed the room, taking care not to slam the door behind him, and made his way down the narrow stairs he'd climbed since he was a wee lad. Within minutes his second in command stood before him as summoned. A year younger than Darach, Hamish's prematurely gray hair left him looking older. The two had grown up together, watching one another's backs, forging a friendship deeper than that of a laird and his clansman. Darach trusted Hamish like a brother.

"There's a lass in my bed," Darach said.

Hamish cocked his head to one side. "Do you find her comely?"

Darach didn't know exactly what he thought about the woman. She lacked the striking beauty of some, but there was something about her that unleashed a yearning in him he'd never before known. "She's fair enough."

"Then what are ye doin' standin' here with me?" Hamish grinned.

"I'm wantin' to know how a stranger to these parts managed to slip past everyone in this house and find her way to my bed."

Hamish's grin faded. "None of the men have reported anyone."

"Exactly."

"Do you want me to send someone to fetch her or should I get her myself?"

"No. Leave her be."

"But—"

"I said leave her be and mention her to no one." His people were a suspicious lot and with them preparing to march on the English crown…. "Having a strange woman show up would unsettle things for sure. Let me give her some thought."

Hamish nodded, his gray hair glinting in the light from the sconce. "Where does she say she is from?"

"A place I have never heard of." He passed a weary hand over his forehead. For a heartbeat he pondered that he might have conjured her in his mind. Nay, the sweet press of her flesh beneath his had been real enough. The confusion and anger darkening her green eyes, her galloping heartbeat beneath him all spoke to a woman of honeyed breath rather than some figment of his imagination.

"And where is she now?" Hamish asked.

"In my bed, where she'll stay until I decide what I'm going to do with her. I promised her passage home tomorrow, but until I'm certain she isna a Sassenach spy, she will stay. Her name is British enough. Kate Wexford." It sounded foreign on his tongue. His conscience didn't quibble at the change of plans. His first responsibility lay in protecting his people. Even so, the thought of her ripe curves beneath his plaid stirred his blood and various and sundry parts. "And I know what I'll be doin' with her soon enough."

"What if she isn't wanting a tumble?"

He hadn't thought of that, he'd just thought they hadn't made it that far yet. "I have yet to bed a lass less than willing."

"And you ken she's willing?"

He had yet to meet a woman who wasn't. "Figure it out for yourself man. She was in my bed with no clothes on."

"I would ken she's willing."

The memory of her pale skin against his plaid

stirred his blood. A few bonnie words and the lass would be his for the tumbling. He smiled at Hamish. "Or she will be soon enough."

KATE AWOKE, instantly alert. There was a lot to be said for the efficacy of power napping she'd perfected as a resident. She knew without glancing about that the Darach MacTavish wannabe was gone—knew it because she didn't *feel* him in the room.

What to do? How to get out of here? The problem was the man could return at any moment. She needed help. She needed to let someone know where she was, which she didn't exactly know, or at least that she'd been taken against her will. She pulled out her cell phone. It was still on, but there wasn't a signal. Dammit. How could they have whisked her away to a place so remote there was no cell phone signal? Marc Fredericks was pulling a stint with Doctors Without Borders in Zimbabwe and even he had cell service. In freaking Zimbabwe, nonetheless.

Calm. Stay calm. She pulled out and turned on her Blackberry. She waited, but no signal bars showed. What the…? She'd paid a boatload of money for guaranteed service. She had it in writing. The only way she shouldn't have an Internet signal was if all the satellites were down and that was a technological impossibility.

Exasperated and slightly panicked she stood and went to the window, trying to get her bearings, shivering at the constant draft in the room. The night sky blanketed the earth with an incredible display of stars. She realized she must be about three or four stories up because she could literally see for miles. With a dawning sense of dismay she realized the stars shone so bright because they weren't competing with street lights. They weren't competing with any lights. For as far as she could see, which she estimated to be several miles from this vantage point, there were no lights other than the odd pinprick which seemed to be more in keeping with a campfire than a streetlight.

And where were the trees? Every landscape within a several hour drive of Atlanta boasted a canopy of trees but all she saw was rolling hills, desolate and barren in the starlight.

She turned from the window, suddenly feeling frantic. Ohmigod. The picture. The picture from the museum. She'd missed it earlier because it had been out of her line of vision. It was the same, the exact same portrait. At least it looked the same. Okay. Definitely weird. And staring at the picture wouldn't get her any answers. If she'd fallen through it to get here, ostensibly she should be able to fall through it to get back home. She walked over and tried to keep going. Ow! She bounced off of the picture and the stone wall. That hurt. And she was still here. Damn.

She methodically checked the stone wall. No electrical outlets surreptitiously tucked behind furniture to keep the authenticity of the room. Nope. They simply weren't there. No central heating and air-conditioning vents. No phone jacks. No nothing except stone walls and floors and a fireplace nearly big enough for her to stand in and a constant draft of cold air. Dread slid down her spine and she pulled the soft wool more tightly around her.

She straightened her back and squared her shoulders, drawing herself up to her full five feet and five-and-a-half inches. Clearly, this room held no answers. She forced herself to walk to the wooden door cut into the stone wall.

She ignored the sick feeling in the pit of her stomach. How many times had she watched scary movies and seen the heroine doing something stupid like opening the door to explore when sure as heck something awful awaited her on the other side? But she had to find out what was going on and her only hope was in discovering what lay out *there*.

She grasped the rustic metal latch and opened it. Just like in the movies, it swung wide with an accompanying *screech,* not exactly what she needed to settle her nerves.

Cold and inky black swallowed her. A musty dankness permeated the chill. Kate hesitated, her nerve nearly deserting her. She clutched the material around her, finding an odd comfort in the man's scent clinging to the fabric.

Stairs went up and down in the narrow winding case. Obviously she was in some sort of turret. This just sucked. She wasn't some princess. She hadn't been sitting around waiting on her prince to show. There was no prince. And Darach MacTavish was too raw, too much man to be prince material.

She balanced herself along the wall with her right hand and edged her way along the staircase. The cold stone floor freezing against her bare feet, she used her toes to feel over the fairly sharp edge of the stone to the next step. Within seconds, the narrow, curving steps and wall obliterated the meager light from the open bedroom door. But even with her pisspoor sense of direction, she wasn't likely to get lost with up and down as her only options.

She heard him, smelled him, felt him to her core before she met him in the dark. Not wanting to send them both tumbling down the narrow winding stairs she whispered into the quiet. "MacTavish?"

"Did you miss me that much, Katie-love, that ye had to come looking for me?"

No one called her Katie and certainly no one in their right mind called her Katie-love, but she was in a situation she neither understood nor controlled and he seemed to be in charge so she supposed he could call her whatever struck his fancy. And she didn't miss the dark note of displeasure underlying his seemingly light remark.

"I was simply trying to get my bearings."

"And I suppose you missed my suggestion you keep to my room." He moved a step closer and his body heat enveloped her. There was nowhere to go. His fingers traced the line of her jaw, down the length of her throat to the ridge of her collarbone. He brushed his thumb against her wildly beating pulse. "Or mebbe you wanted me to tie you to my bed. Is that it Katie-love?"

He feathered his hands along her shoulders, down her arms and gently captured her wrists. He raised them above her head and pinned them against the wall with one hand. Cold, rough-hewn stones bit into her shoulders and arms. His hand, callused but warm, cupped her neck and he traced a sensual pattern with his thumb against her throat.

Her breath lodged in her chest, caught up in the mad beating of her heart. Was it him, or the dark, or the situation that heightened her senses? For more than a month, she'd smelled his scent each time she'd visited the museum, and now it evoked the same response, but tenfold. He had her pinned to the wall in a strange place and still a dark, sensual heat coursed through her.

He lowered his head and his hair teased against her bare shoulder. His warm breath danced over her skin. His lips whispered against her, not quite a kiss, over her shoulder, along the line where his plaid covered her breasts. Instinctively she arched her back bringing her closer to his mouth. "Ah, that's some fine skin you have Katie-love, soft and warm and you smell good too." He nuzzled where her shoulder met her neck and Kate thought she might melt at the feel of his lips against her skin, the faint scrape of his whiskers. "It could fair drive a man mad to wonder if you're that soft and smell that good all over. I would like to say all the men would be fair and noble were they to run into you wearing naught but a plaid, but that's not the case. There are many who'd be driven to seek what you hide beneath and none too particular as to your willingness. So, if you won't keep yourself safe, I'll do what I have to do. As laird of Glenagan, it's my job to look after my people." He slid his hands down her arms, leaving a trail of fire in his wake.

"But I'm not your people." Her protest, which she fully intended to be forceful and assertive, somehow got lost in the sensation of his fingers against her bare arms, and came out a hoarse whisper.

He wrapped an arm, much like a band of steel, about her waist. Before she realized what he was up to, he hoisted her off her feet and over one massive shoulder. "Ah, Katie-love, that's where you are wrong. As long as you're on my land, you belong to me."

3

DARACH MACTAVISH was confounded. Ever since he was a wee lad, the lasses had taken a ken to him. So, finding a lass in his bed hadn't been that surprising. Finding her as bare as a bairn had been something of a boon. But she didn't seem wont to stay there and that was confounding, as was her strange speech.

He tested the last knot. Katie wouldn't be going anywhere until he decided she should. He looked down at her stony face. "If you're uncomfortable, you have no one but yourself to blame."

She turned her face to the wall, away from him without answering.

"Ye left me no choice. At least I didna bind your legs." She seemed in no mood for a tumble and to have her on his bed with her legs spread, her ankles bound to the corner posts…well, he didn't need the temptation.

"Thank you." She looked at him, anger simmering beneath her stony facade. "You're wasting both of our time. Obviously you've confused me with someone else. People will miss me and the authorities will look for me, but no one will pay you a penny for me."

"You think I want to ransom you?"

"Why else are you tying me up? Why won't you let me leave?"

"I've told you why, you daft lass."

"I'm not daft, you jackass…at least I don't think I am. I just want to go home." The last word ended on an abrupt note. Was it because she was about to start caterwauling or because she'd said too much?

"Were you perhaps meeting someone to take you home?" He should've thought of that before. Of course she wasn't here alone. Finally, the situation made sense. "Were you sent here to distract me? Who were you on your way to meet? Where were you meeting them?"

A hint of bewilderment lurked behind the frustration in her green eyes. "I don't know why I'm here. I wish I did. No, that's not true. I don't care why I'm here. I just want to wake up and have this dream over."

Her nonsense held a note of truth. But it was, in fact nonsense, and he pressed her. "Tell me where you're to meet your people and I'll take you there. As long as no harm comes to a MacTavish on this night, I'll set you and your people free. It's a generous offer and one I won't grant again, so make your decision wisely, Katie Wexford."

"I wish I could tell you what you want to know. I would if I could. I'm not stoic or heroic or any of those things. I want a hot shower, a glass of red wine, my silk pajamas and my bed. This—" she glanced around the room and then pointedly at him, "—is not my idea of a good evening."

Darach crossed to the door. He'd rouse the whole castle. Better to surprise the enemy than be caught unaware. And he'd spent entirely too much of his time talking with this woman. He turned to face her. "I am going to rouse the castle. If your people are here, we'll find them and you can trust they'll be shown no mercy. Know that you brought this upon them. Know that you could have saved them and chose to do nothing. Know their blood to be on your hands."

She nodded. "I'll be here when you get back."

By all that was holy, she either spoke the truth or was as touched as they came.

"GATHER THE MEN and ready them to search the castle," Darach said.

Hamish stood before his laird for the second time that evening and sighed to himself. Darach had been in a state earlier and in no mood for the only explanation he, Hamish could offer. Hamish had held out a slight hope that Darach and the lass might figure it out on their own, but he'd feared it might come to this. His laird and friend, Darach was a strong decisive personality. And even though Hamish had only a faint, general impression of the woman he'd shoved through the portrait, she was undoubtedly made of equally stern stuff. Hamish wished this next part was over with. It promised to be difficult.

"Is this about the strange lass in your bed? I take it she wasn't up for a tumble?"

"I caught her coming down the stairs after I had told her to stay in my room. I think she was on her way to meet someone. That or she's been sent as a distraction. Now, gather the men."

Hamish stood before him without doing his bidding, searching for a way to break his news to Darach. God's tooth this was going to be awkward. Hamish should've already prepared for this. Darach glanced sharply at him. "Time is wasting man."

"I would like to meet the woman. I think I can explain."

"I thought you had seen no one enter the castle."

Hamish was almost positive it was the same woman, but she'd shown up without her clothes? "Let me meet her."

"And what if we're bluidy well overrun while you're up visiting with her?"

"Trust me. Have I ever offered you unwise counsel? Take me to her."

Hamish regarded the man he'd known and loved like a brother his entire life. More than once he'd entrusted Darach with his life. Hamish hoped he'd do the same now.

Darach turned abruptly and made his way toward the keep. Hamish followed, leaving behind his customary banter, scrambling to decide how best to present the situation to Darach and the lass. It was so much easier when those involved figured it out on their own.

They entered the room, Darach first. The woman spoke. "That was quick. I told you I wasn't meeting anyone." Hamish stepped around Darach and smiled a greeting.

Recognition widened her eyes. "You—you... you're the one who shoved me into the painting. I know it. You're younger, but I recognize you. I don't know what kind of game you're playing but I want out."

"You brought her here?" Darach reared back, betrayal echoing in his stance. "I asked and—"

"I told you none of the men saw her enter and they didn't. Hear me out and know it is a strange enough tale I have to tell."

Kate spoke up from the bed. "Okay. We're finally getting somewhere and while you're telling it, how about you untie me."

Darach looked from Hamish to Kate and shook his head in distrust. "Not until I have heard the tale."

"The first manner of business would be that this is indeed Glenagan, Scotland and it is November of 1744," Hamish said with an apologetic smile at Kate.

The woman's skin grew paler still at his words, all the blood seeming to drain from her body. She should thank Darach that she was flat on her back, else she might have fallen.

"No." She breathed the single word through clenched lips.

"Who is she?" Darach asked.

Where was a good place to start? Experience had taught him there were no good places to start with this. "She's a woman from two hundred and sixty years, well two hundred sixty two years to be precise, in the future."

Darach eyed him as if madness had overcome him.

"Ah. I see you think I've gone a might daft and for sure it is a bit hard to believe." He looked at Darach to show him neither madness nor deception shadowed his eyes. "She is from Georgia, a place that today is a colony of the crown and the city she comes from does not yet exist. She is not British. She and her people are known as Americans."

"She said you brought her here. So, I'm supposed to believe you are still alive two hundred sixty two years in the future?"

Hamish shrugged. "I told you it's a strange tale."

"But you haven't been gone from the castle."

"I don't know how to explain it, but I exist on several different planes, at different points in time, in different places."

"Are you some kind of dark magic?"

"I don't know what I am." He'd ceased long ago to feel sorrow over his unusual state. "I've just learned to accept it. I can't *make* anything happen. But things happen *through* me." He gestured to the painting on the wall. "That painting spoke to you, drew you, did it not, lass?"

"Yes." Her skin flushed to a rosy glow.

"You've seen that painting before?" Darach asked her.

"Yes. It was in a traveling exhibit, Sex Through the Ages, in the Atlanta museum."

"Sex Through the Ages?" Darach frowned at her.

"I didn't name the thing," Kate snapped back at him. "I just showed up for the viewing."

Hamish jumped in to get the conversation back

on track. "And the draw was so strong you couldn't stay away?"

"Yes. Did you do that to me? Did you cast some kind of spell?"

"No. What you felt was between the two of you. That's the way it works. I don't pick anyone. If you weren't supposed to be here, if on some level you didn't want to be here, you wouldn't."

"Wait a second. Something's obviously gotten screwed up somewhere along the line. I definitely don't *want* to be here. I want to be home. You've got the wrong gal. I think you meant to snag my friend Jordan. She's a history major. Trust me. She'd much rather be here, well, maybe not tied to the bed," she glared in Darach's direction, "but she's into history and this would be right up her alley. Trust me on this. I'm not the person for this. I don't do history. I've never even been to the Renaissance festival 'cause I don't like that stuff. I'm a techno freak. I love the conveniences of modern life. Electricity. Running water. Flush toilets. CAT scans. Penicillin. Starbucks."

"Aye. A mocha latte grande is a thing of beauty."

"See. You understand. You have to send me back."

He upended his palms in a gesture of helplessness. "I can not. Only you can send yourself back."

"No. That's not true. 'Cause I'd be home right

now if I could. And I tried to go through the picture earlier."

"No, lass, 'tis yourself that has brought you here. You wanted to be here so much you were willing to come as bare as a bairn. And once you have taken care of what you came here for, you'll return."

Darach stood, arrogant, commanding, smug. "So the lass wanted a tumble with me that bad, did she?"

"Actually, *your* need for *her* was so strong that she felt it coming through."

"Now I know you are daft, man. I don't need her." He eyed her stretched out on his bed, clad in his plaid. "Now, there is no denying I want her. I'm willing to tumble a comely lass, but I don't need her. There is any number of lasses willing to warm my bed."

"You are the most arrogant, pig-headed, macho, blustering bag of hot air. Whatever faint glimmer of attraction I felt at one point for a man in a picture has totally dissipated having experienced your lack of charm first-hand."

Darach's mouth tightened. "Aye. And I can do without a viper-tongued wench."

"Wench? *Wench?* Lass is one thing, but did you just call me a wench? I'll have you know I'm a doctor. No one calls me a wench. I passed my boards with flying colors. I could take you apart and put you back together with my eyes closed."

"That may all be well and true, Katie-love, but while you are here, I'm the laird."

Hamish let himself out of the room. For the time being, his work was done.

4

___

"Now, DO YOU THINK you can untie me?" Kate said. "I can prove to you I'm from the twenty-first century."

As fantastical concept as it was, she was convinced she'd somehow time traveled. The old guy who now looked young and satellite absence had made a believer of her. However, she thought that business about her wanting to be here was a load of horse manure. In no way, shape, form or fashion did she *want* to be here.

Maybe that conductor guy had smoked some crack. Did they have crack in 1744? She knew virtually nothing about historic mind-altering drugs. For that matter, she knew precious little about historic anything. It wasn't her deal.

"I will unbind you if I have your word you'll remain in this room, otherwise, for your own good, I'll keep you bound to my bed." He stood at the end of the bed, strong legs braced apart, thick arms crossed over his massive chest.

He wasn't blustering. He was giving her a choice. She didn't doubt for a moment he could and would keep her tied to the bed if she didn't cooperate. In fact, she could scream herself silly and it wouldn't matter. He was in charge and no one would cross him. She didn't have to know jack about history to know that. She recognized absolute power and in this world, Darach MacTavish was literally a law unto himself.

"I promise. I'll stay in this room."

He moved with a grace uncommon to a man of his size and knelt on the bed. Sensation fluttered low in her belly. His scent, the same that had drawn her over and over again for the past several weeks, was even more potent and alluring up close and personal. Dark hair was sprinkled tantalizingly along his legs and forearms, and she knew for a certain, blood-stirring fact that he was naked beneath his kilt. Muscles corded in his arms as he worked loose the knot binding her left hand. His hair swung forward, a dark curtain drawn on the harsh line of his nose, the bold line of his jaw, and the sensuous curve of his lips.

His fingers pressed against her wrist and palm as he worked at the knot in the material. She touched people all day, checking pulses, feeling for abnormalities, but this…this was different altogether. Her pulse leapt and tingles spread through her.

Kate flushed at his touch and the heat it evoked. She should look away—study the ceiling and mentally review the last cases she'd seen at work. But she couldn't look away, couldn't redirect her attention because that incredible surge of heat and lust and want drew her to him. It was a yearning born from deep within that surpassed attraction and even will. She didn't want to feel drawn to him. She didn't want to ache for more of his touch.

The fabric gave way, releasing her wrist...until he recaptured it in his hands. He stroked her pulse point, performing a sensual massage with his thumb. "I hope it didna hurt you." The low timbre of his voice thrummed through her. He looked at her and there was no denying the heat smoldering in his gaze. Without looking away, he slowly brought her wrist to his mouth until his warm breath whispered against her flesh.

Her heart thundered in her chest. She ought to snatch her hand away but, God help her, she wanted to know the feel of that exquisitely sensual mouth against her skin. Wanted to know if the inherent promise in those well-shaped lips was real or merely fantasy's fodder.

He pressed a kiss to her wrist and sweet heat poured through her. He nuzzled and suckled the flesh as if he were savoring a delicate treat. Instinctively she curled her fingers against his cheek. He lifted his head. "You would think me naught but a brutish Highlander were I tae bruise you."

She reclaimed her hand and wet her dry lips with the tip of her tongue. "I'm fine. If you would just untie my other hand now."

"As you wish, Katie-love." She fully expected him to walk around to the other side of the bed. Instead, Darach MacTavish, with a wicked smile, climbed atop and straddled her. Powerful thighs braced on either side of her, he leaned forward and worked at the other knot.

What she'd felt outside that portrait now increased exponentially. She was wantonly, wickedly aware that except for two soft bits of cloth, she and this magnificent male specimen were naked. The heavy length of him pressed against her hip as he leaned over her. Stretched above her at the angle he was, the scar she'd daydreamed about earlier was slightly visible.

She reached up and traced her finger down the puckered line marring his back. His skin was warm and supple on either side of the scar's hard ridge. Did she imagine the small shudder that ran through him?

"That must have hurt."

He straightened and despite his arrogant grin, his

eyes held the same hard glint they had when she'd made her stupid Queen of England quip. "'Twas just a scratch. I found the wrong end of a sword."

"How were you stitched up?" Her training left her curious. She was certain it wasn't a couple of shots of Lidocaine to numb it and then vicryl and ethilon sutures to close it up.

"We were a night's ride from Glenagan. My father poured a measure of whiskey in it and then sewed it back together with horsehair."

Whiskey in an open wound of that size must have been excruciating. "And you rode the next day?"

He shrugged. "We had a pressing need to get back. Sima applied a poultice when I returned and it was nary a problem. I was but a lad and healed quickly."

He'd released her other wrist, absently rubbing her flesh. Kate needed to get herself out of this situation—both the immediate situation of being flat on her back with Braveheart sending her into a hormonal meltdown and the situation of having lost a century or two. And that meant focusing on something other than this man's powerful thighs braced on either side of her legs, the shattering slide of his fingers against her skin, his scent, the fact that she was in his bed.

She swallowed and tried to project the decisive,

I'm-in-charge voice that worked so well in the ER. "I'd like to get up now that you've untied me."

He shifted off of her without saying anything but his arrogant smile spoke volumes, telling her he knew exactly how he affected her.

She stood and double-checked the knot holding her makeshift toga-kilt in place. "The sooner we can figure out how to get me back to where I belong and out of your hair, the better."

KATIE WEXFORD CROSSED to stand before the waning fire and dug in her satchel. To be certain, it'd be much simpler if she weren't here, but he didn't want her gone. Yet. He'd thought to taunt her when he'd straddled her but he'd been effectively hoisted by his own petard. Her skin had felt like the finest wool beneath his fingertips. Her skin had tasted like a draught of the smoothest whiskey that lit a fire in his belly and left him wanting more.

Even if she was touched. And Hamish seemed to have caught her madness. But 'twas a fact that the daft were touched by God and it was his job to protect both Kate and Hamish, now more than ever. Best to humor them both until he could decide on a plan of action.

But 'twas also obvious Kate and Hamish were not strangers. Were it any other man, he'd have them both under guard. But more than once Hamish had proven himself loyal and trustworthy. Twice he'd covered Darach's back in a skirmish when a dagger finding its home would have made Hamish laird since Darach had no offspring. Nay, perhaps both Kate and Hamish suffered from a fever that had affected their reasoning.

He followed her and tossed more peat onto the fire. The flickering light danced across her naked shoulders and the length of her neck bared by her shorn hair. Her scent, clean and fresh, like the moor on a sunny day, stirred his senses. Mayhap he was in danger of catching the same fever to be affected this way by a daft lass.

Footsteps pounded up the stone stairs and Hamish burst into the room carrying a young lad of no more than five. The lad, son of Anice and Grahame, lay still, his eyes closed, his face blue, water dripping from his hair and body. Hamish's chest heaved and he spoke between great gulps of air. "I found…the lad…in the burn. Ye'll have to tell his parents. Anice will near grieve herself to death."

"Give me the boy," the woman said, freeing the knot and yanking off the MacTavish plaid as she spoke, leaving herself naked once again.

The woman was truly mad.

"For God's sake, I'm a doctor. This is what I do. Give him to me. I think I can save him."

Without waiting and without regard for her naked state, she wrapped the plaid about the child and placed him on the floor. Without pause, she bent and blew a breath into his mouth. Again she repeated the action. The third time around, the lad retched water and blinked his eyes open.

By all that was holy…the lad had been dead and now he was alive. "What kind of magic are you?"

The woman looked at him with a mixture of exasperation and disgust. "It's not magic. It's medicine. I told you, I'm a doctor and that's called resuscitation." She smoothed a hand over the child's brow. "He'll be fine." She stood and looked at Hamish. "Get him into dry clothes and let him sleep a while."

Hamish left with the lad and Darach dug out yet another plaid for Katie. He studied her anew as she once again wrapped herself in the red and blue MacTavish colors.

"You saved the lad." She had truly reacted as a healer.

"It's what I'm trained to do. Anyone from my time period trained in basic rescue could've done the same," she said.

Could it be possible? Was Hamish speaking the truth? Could it be so that Hamish wasn't simply daft and the woman had come from the future? It could not be so.

Kate picked her satchel up from the floor where she'd dropped it when Hamish had entered. "I can see you're still not convinced I am who I say I am." She dug in the satchel and pulled out a card. "Here. It's my driver's license." She handed him a card and pointed to a date. "There's my birthdate." Darach excelled at sums. He was two hundred and sixty-four years older than Kate Wexford.

What the devil was this? It was a portrait of her, yet not a portrait. "What kind of portrait is this?"

"It's a picture. A photograph." She shrugged, her palms upright. "I'm not sure when photography was invented. Obviously later than this."

He studied the card. It didn't do her justice. Short flaxen hair curled about her face. Wide green eyes with a hint of a frown marring her brow stared at him from the portrait. No smile lifted the corners of her full mouth. It did nothing to capture her wry humor and resilience. "Well, you're more comely than this. I hope you didn't pay much for the rendering."

Her smile stopped just short of a laugh. "Thanks... I think. The DMV isn't much into glamour shots."

He had no idea what a DMV or a glamour shot was but he supposed it didn't matter. What mattered was that he was only about two hundred sixty-four years older than her. And he'd never seen anything like what she called a photograph.

He no longer doubted Hamish. He'd only ever known him to speak the truth and it appeared that it was truth rather than madness. Except the notion that he, Darach, needed this woman and that was why she was here. Her scent teased him, as did the gleam of light on her skin. He'd not deny he wanted her, but there was a world of difference between want and need. He'd wanted women and had them, but he'd never needed them.

"It explains much—your strange accent and manner of speech, your hair—but not why you are here."

Kate glanced up from returning her card to her satchel. "I assure you I don't want to be here, regardless of what Hamlet said."

He'd be damned if she didn't glare at him as if *he* was to blame for her being here. "It's Hamish and might I remind you that you're the one who showed up naked in my bed."

She tilted her head at a haughty angle and stared down the length of her nose at him. "A gallant man wouldn't have pointed that out and trust me, I want to be back home."

He laughed and knew it held a mocking note. He took a step closer to her. "But you were attracted to me in that painting?" He could feel it now, like some force beneath the inky waters of a loch, something deep and strong between them, something potent beneath the surface.

She blinked, looking up at him and in that moment, he recognized an answering flash of acknowledgement in her eyes. "Yes, I'll admit I was attracted to you when I saw the painting." She smiled with a sweetness he didn't trust. "Of course, that was before your personality factored into it."

Darach threw back his head and laughed. Mayhap she had a strange way with words, but her meaning was clear. Ah, but he was enjoying himself with Katie Wexford. Most of the lasses fair swooned over him. Certainly none had complained about his personality. And he thought Katie was not being exactly truthful. He reached out and tested a measure of her hair between his fingers. Her eyes widened and her lips parted. With great care he tucked the curl behind her well-shaped ear, his fingers lingering against the delicate shell. Her swift intake of breath echoed the pounding of his heart. "Aye, so that means you do not fancy me now?"

She wet her lower lip with the tip of her tongue and lust knotted his gut. "Not particularly," she said. Her breathy tone belied her words.

Aye. She was lying. She wanted him as much as he wanted her and it wasn't arrogance on his part. It wasn't fear that left her trembling at his slightest touch. There was fire between them and if he had unraveled this correctly, she needed to admit it. He skimmed his palm over her bare shoulder and heat raced through him. "More's the pity."

She held her ground, despite the shiver he felt run through her, and narrowed her eyes at him. "Why do you say that?"

He rested his hands on the smoothness of her bare shoulders, her skin warm and soft beneath his callused palms. He curled his fingers against her sweet flesh. "Because it seems to me that it was lust that brought you here…"

"Perhaps."

"Then it stands to reason that if you satisfy that lust, you should go back to where you came from."

"Congratulations! That's probably the strangest pick-up line I've ever heard. And I don't think so."

"I'm just trying to help you out, Katie-love." He bracketed her shoulders with his hands, her skin soft beneath his palms.

She shrugged off his touch. "That's terribly generous of you."

He trailed one finger down her arm. "I'm known for my generosity."

"Uh-huh. I'll just bet you are." She swatted his hand away.

Satisfied that she wanted him, he smiled at her, crossing his arms over his chest. "I'm just trying to help you get back to where you want to be."

KATE PACED to the other side of the room. Not only did pacing help her think, but it got her out of Darach MacTavish's immediate vicinity, which was a bonus in the being able to think department.

Maybe she'd told a little white lie—okay, a whopping white lie—when she said she wasn't as attracted to him as she had been. It was more a matter of she shouldn't be as attracted to him as she had been. But here she'd met this man, under circumstances beyond weird, and he was proposing they have sex? She didn't think so.

She took a deep breath and her practical side kicked in. Wasn't she bringing twenty-first century mores to a situation where they didn't exactly belong? What were they going to do? Go out to dinner a couple of times? Go to a movie and perhaps a night out at the museum to get to know one another better?

What was the courting ritual in eighteenth-century Scotland? Damn if she knew. And she didn't want to be courted, she just wanted to go home.

For one panic-inducing moment the thought crept in that she might not be able to get back home. What then? What if she was stuck here? No! She refused to think that way. And maybe Darach Mac-Tavish was on to something. She knew for certain she didn't want to hang out here any longer than necessary.

She liked the twenty-first century. No, that wasn't true. She loved the twenty-first century. And she'd worked too damn hard to get that assistant appointment. She wasn't about to lose her job because she'd been squandering time in the past. And she supposed if she was going to have sex, there were worse specimens out there than the one before her. It probably wouldn't be too bad—if she could just get him to keep his mouth shut.

And much as she didn't want to think in the direction of being stuck here, if she was stuck here for more than a couple of hours, being the chief's lover was probably the safest position to take. But could she just turn off all her years of upbringing and hop in bed with a man who was essentially a stranger? She knew some women fantasized about stuff like this. She wasn't one of them. She just didn't know if she had it in her.

"Maybe you're right. Maybe sex together is the key."

The bastard actually laughed. "I've seen men more enthusiastic who were about to be hung."

"I'm in a different freaking century and I have no clue whether I'm actually going to make it back to where I want to be. You're a stranger and I'm supposed to be jumping up and down at the prospect of having sex with you?" Bottom line, she was scared. Nearly spitless. "I'm sure sex with strangers is nothing new to you, but it's not part of my regimen."

All the arrogance and amusement vanished, replaced by a kindness she hadn't noted before. "I think things are very different where you come from, I'm sure of it. But no, few strangers show up in these parts and those that do, I don't bed as a rule." He reached out and drew her to him, but it was a gesture of comfort, an offer of protection, which felt almost as foreign to Kate as sex with a stranger. "This must be a terrible situation to find yourself in, Katie-love. We won't take any more action tonight. Rest and on the morn we'll work on this."

"What happens in the meantime, if tomorrow it doesn't work? You said earlier the women would stone me and the men would…" she stumbled, not wanting to even give voice to the possibilities he'd mentioned.

"You have my word that I'll let no harm come to

you. I give you my oath as the laird of Glenagan. No man or woman will dare to cross me on this. You will be protected or I'll die trying."

"Why would you do that for me?"

"Because I have never known Hamish to tell less than the truth and he says I'm the reason you're here which makes you my responsibility and makes it my duty to protect and get you back where you belong without harm befalling you."

She studied his face. It was a strong, bold face that bespoke harshness, yet his eyes reflected honesty and integrity. Kate was very good at compartmentalizing, it was a necessary aspect of her job, but she wasn't good at masking what she thought and felt. Could she trust him? What other option did she have but to trust him? He seemed to read her doubt.

"You'll come to no harm while you are here. And tonight you'll find nothing but sleep in my bed. I can offer you naught but my word and you can do naught but trust me."

HE WAS A FOOL and then some. Mayhap she hadn't been overly eager but he'd not have been forcing her had he bedded her earlier. He could have had a bit of sport and then she could've returned home and he wouldn't be laying here now, tortured by her scent, her soft curves pressed against him, wrapped in his plaid.

He considered taking care of the situation. He could ease his lips against hers, the tenderest of kisses that would slowly rouse her from slumber. Kisses that would suckle the fullness of her lower lip, that would cull the honey of her mouth. Kisses that would steal beneath her hesitation and release the heat he'd sensed. Then he could slide his hand beneath the plaid and ease her legs apart. He could pluck and strum and play her like a lyre until she was fair ready for him. Then he'd ease his rod into her and they'd be about the business that would set both their worlds to rights. But he'd given his word that they'd wait until the morn.

Kate sighed in her sleep and threw one arm up over her head, threatening to spill one breast over the edge of the MacTavish tartan. Darach sighed and crossed his arms over his chest. There'd be no relieving the ache in his loins tonight. No, his bluidy mouth had taken care of that. He supposed he was glad Katie Wexford was getting a good night's sleep. One of them might as well.

DARACH STOMPED INTO the courtyard in a fine temper the following morning. He should've tumbled the lass last night and been done with it. Then mayhap he'd have gotten some sleep instead of stewing about in his own lust til morn. He made straight for Hamish.

Hamish didn't bother to hide his grin. "I see a night with your lass did nothing to sweeten your temper."

Darach scowled. "She is a bluidy thorn in my side."

"Hmph. I'd have guessed a thorn in another part."

"When you're done with your jest, I need answers."

Hamish sobered and shook his head. "You won't find them from me. I would if I could, but I don't know. It's the way I told you last eve, I don't make decisions. I didn't pick her. You picked her. I just get a sense of who and when. She wouldn't be here if she was not supposed to be here."

"So you said. And since she was naked in my bed, we both decided that 'twas lust that brought her here and taking care of that should send her back."

Hamish held his hands, palm up, in a helpless gesture. "Sounds reasonable to me. But if it's want of a tumble that brought her here and a good tumble that will send her back, why do you look so sour? Since when has that curried a frown?" Darach glared at him and Hamish began to laugh. "You didn't, did yae?"

Darach raked an exasperated hand through his hair. "She was nervous. Strange place. Strange man. Strange century."

"You are a good man, Darach MacTavish."

"I'm a bluidy foolish man." He scrubbed a hand

across his jaw. "I shouldna let the night pass. I think I've finally convinced her to stay put and out of sight but I don't think she understands what could happen to her if she was caught outside of the castle." The Highlands were a wild and dangerous place and 'twas often difficult to know which man was friend and which was foe.

"It's been two years and we haven't had another incident with the bastards."

"Aye. But I think it's just a matter of time. And we all know. Our women don't go unattended and our men are prepared when they go with them."

Two years and hatred for the English still burned a black hole in his soul. Two years he'd lived with his cousin Ian losing his bride Moragh to marauding dragoons who'd considered a Scots lass a bit of sport.

They'd bound Ian to a tree and taken turns raping Moragh in front of her husband. They'd left her on the ground like a piece of offal. Beautiful Moragh of the red hair and bright green eyes had died afterward.

Ian not only lost his wife that day, he'd gone daft and grieved himself to death and the clan MacTavish had learned a painful, costly lesson. No Scotsman was safe as long as that Hanoverian dog sat on the British throne. Not only was Bonnie Prince Charlie the rightful king, but without him, Scotland's fate seemed grim indeed.

It had become increasingly clear to both of them that Scotland's salvation lay in seeing Charles sit the throne. As they had discussed more than once, Darach's hesitation in swearing his fealty to the cause had been the lack of a clear plan as to accomplish that feat.

"I won't have another woman raped on my watch and I won't take what she is not willing to give." As laird, it was his right to take what he wanted. He knew of those that did, but Darach was not of that ilk. "I have no need of a woman who's not eager and willing to spread her legs for me."

"And have you ever met one?"

"I did last night." The hair stood on the nape of his neck and heat collided through him. He glanced toward the solar window. He couldn't see her, but he could feel her. She was there, watching him. He knew it as clearly as if she'd called to him by name. He glanced at the storm gathering in the distance, across the moor. "There's a storm coming."

"So it would seem."

"I'm going up there now. She is up and awake."

"And you know this how?"

Was he going to announce to Hamish that he could feel her looking at him? That he seemed to have a connection...a sense...about this woman he'd never experienced with anyone else. He didn't think he'd divulge that bit of vulnerability to Hamish.

Not only did he dislike the feeling of vulnerability, it wasn't safe for Katie either. Those close to men in his position, lairds who inherited the care of the clan, were often used as pawns.

Power could be a dangerous thing. Those that didn't have it wanted it. And he'd much rather be the one in power than the one without, but often those that coveted it, didn't realize the price extracted and the responsibilities that came hand in hand with it.

But he'd felt her fear, her apprehension last night. Just the way he felt her watching him now. "I'm just guessing she's up now. And I don't trust her to stay put. I have no idea how long this is going to take but I'm going to do my best to send her home. Allow no one to disturb me."

"And what shall I tell anyone who asks?"

His people were a curious lot, for sure. And he couldna blame them. Curiosity was the mark of a MacTavish. And he was curious enough as to how she tasted, what her scent would be like with his mark on her, what she'd feel like, look like, with him deep inside her, the way she'd sound when he brought her to satisfaction. He fair burned with the need to sate his curiosity. "Tell them I have a fever."

5

KATE STOOD AT THE WINDOW and buried her face in the soft wool that bore the scent she'd come to associate with sexual arousal, the scent that she'd first known from a painting. Darach MacTavish's. It was still a fantastical concept that her practical mind found difficult to embrace but—she glanced around her at the turret room complete with stone walls and a definite lack of twenty-first century amenities—this definitely wasn't Atlanta, Georgia.

Of course that had been painfully apparent when she'd woken with a full bladder and finally found a chamber pot in the other corner. There was a lot to be said for flush toilets. She'd popped a piece of spearmint gum from her purse in her mouth in lieu of a toothbrush.

Dark clouds scudded across the dark sky, unrelieved by even a glimmer of sunlight. She had no clue what time it was and it was harder still to gauge the time with the heavy cloud cover.

Far below, people moved about. Men, women, children and an assortment of animals. Sheep, chickens, duck, was that an oxen? She made sure to stay back, out of sight. If she didn't need to go traipsing about on her own—she took his warning of stoning and rape as real, he didn't seem the type given to exaggeration—she'd surmise she didn't need to advertise her presence by hanging out of a window.

Even with the mix of people below, she immediately spotted Darach. Some of the other men were as tall and their shoulders equally as wide, but he wore an unmistakable air of command. As if he possessed some sixth sense, he glanced up at the window where she stood. He was far below her but she could feel the heat of his gaze, the connection between them even at that distance. He looked away and said something to the man beside him, who she thought must be Hamish but it was difficult to tell at this distance, and then strode toward the castle.

She flushed and anticipation hummed through her, pebbling her nipples against the brush of the plaid.

She had forgotten it until this moment, but she'd dreamed of him last night. Her body felt full and ripe as she recalled the way he'd kissed her. The feel of his mouth against her lips, her breasts, the fullness of him between her thighs. She'd woken and realized it was only a dream because the man had been next to her, but not on her or in her and she'd fallen back to sleep, knowing a vague discontent and a definite ache.

She knew with a certainty that he was on his way up to her. And she knew what he was coming for. Last night he'd said wait until the morning. Morning appeared to be here. He was a stranger and she didn't know him any better than she had last night but she wasn't nearly as reluctant now.

Okay, she wasn't into self-delusion. One, she did know him better than she had last night because she'd learned quite a bit about the man who'd sensed her hesitation and then given and kept his word throughout the night. It also told her something about the laird of Glenagan that he'd left her to sleep this morning when he could've so easily awakened her and done the deed.

And this morning she seemed to have lost her trepidation about intimacy with a sort-of stranger. She wanted to go back to Atlanta and her century in a desperate kind of way and honestly, it had been a long, long time since she'd had sex. She wasn't into casual sex and she wasn't much into relationships because they were messy and potentially devastating and she was busy and well…it just hadn't happened in a long time.

But, if she thought about it rationally, this could be a beautiful thing. He turned her on. She seemed to turn him on. A little togetherness then she'd go back to her century and he'd stay in his and that would take care of any post-coital awkwardness. There wouldn't be any fear that she'd run into him in the hall at the hospital or bump into him at a restaurant.

All things considered, this could be the perfect solution. She discarded her gum into the wrapper and put it back in her purse. She finger combed her hair and was decidedly glad she didn't have a mirror. She really didn't want to know what she looked like without fresh make-up and hair gel. She stood in front of the glowing embers in the grate and waited.

WITHIN MINUTES MACTAVISH entered the room carrying a bowl. He closed the door behind him with a dull thud.

"I thought you might be hungry," he said, proffering the dish.

He didn't just enter a room, he commanded it, filled it with his sheer size and force of presence. Kate's heart beat like a tom-tom in her chest. And she realized that she was in fact hungry.

She took the bowl of what looked like oatmeal and thanked him. She was somewhere this side of ravenous. Taking a bite, she found it surprisingly good. She hadn't expected to like it. She proceeded to finish it in an embarrassingly short amount of time.

She placed the empty bowl on the table to the left of the fire. "Thank you, again."

MacTavish refueled the fire and it blazed to life. Outside, a fury of wind, rain, thunder and lightning lashed at the castle that stood undaunted by the elements. The fire warmed the room and burnished his skin to a golden glow.

He reached out and Kate felt his touch almost before his fingers brushed her flesh. It was as if every nerve ending craved his touch. An ache unlike anything she'd known before welled inside her and she curved her cheek into his hand.

"Your skin is like the finest fabric. You are a woman who was meant to be touched."

She'd never given it any thought. In fact, until now she would've disagreed, but the mere drag of his fingers against her cheek resonated through her. She traced the back of his hand. It was like learning a new terrain—the length of his fingers, the sinewy ridges, the leashed power. The desire burning in his dark eyes came through in his touch.

"I've a terrible hunger for one of your kisses." He said, lowering his head, blocking the light of the fire.

Kate trembled. She'd wanted the man in the picture for weeks. She'd dreamt of him. Now he stood before her, flesh and blood.

Often she felt like an observer. That's what she did at her job. She stood back and directed. That's what she'd done with the picture. She'd wanted him but she'd wanted him as an observer. Now she was no longer standing outside watching. Now she was in the picture and by God if she wasn't standing outside watching, she'd participate to the fullest. She knew she was a bit of an overachiever and this situation was no exception.

This time tomorrow, she'd be waking up in her own bedroom, in her own bed—heck, if this went well, she'd be back home within the hour. There was no need to squander opportunity. And as long as he kept saying stuff like he hungered for her kiss and didn't mention any of that wench stuff, then he didn't necessarily need to keep his mouth shut.

"You fed me when I was hungry. Let me return the favor." She pulled his head down to hers, but it was MacTavish who took control of the kiss. His mouth whispered against hers, the merest brush, a litmus test, and then returned to claim hers. Kate curled her fingers in his dark hair and absorbed the feel of his lips, the warmth of his breath. Like the unfurling of a tight bud, the kiss grew and deepened until Kate was caught up in the sensation of his mouth on hers, the heat of his big hands on her shoulders.

Instead of satisfying their hunger, the kiss intensified it. His tongue swept the recesses of her mouth.

He raised his head. "A man could feast on your mouth all day, Katie-love."

Kate stood there, her mouth still tingling from his kisses. Men didn't say things like this to her on a regular basis, well, okay, they never said anything like this to her and she didn't know how to respond.

"Uh, thank you." She stepped back from him. It was much easier to think that way. "I think we have to have a bit more of a plan than we're working with now." She pointed toward the painting on the wall. "That was the painting I came through to get here. As you recall, that's where I was when I got here. I think we should pick it up from there."

His wicked smile set her pulse hammering. "Aye. Then I suppose I can't make love to you on that sheepskin rug before the fireplace."

Kate hadn't exactly known what to expect from Darach MacTavish, but if he did the rest the way he kissed…. "I have to be home in time for work on Monday, but I'm really not in any big rush. Um… maybe we should work in a practice, you know, just to make sure we get it right." She had the day off.

This beat the heck out of doing laundry. "Unless you have something else to do."

"I've left instructions that I am not to be disturbed."

"For how long?"

"I've instructed Hamish to bring our meals. Otherwise, until I leave this room, no one will dare approach it."

"What would have to be happening for someone to come up here?"

"The castle could be overrun with Sassenach—"

"Who? What?"

"The bluidy English. My men would station themselves at the stairs below, but none would come up here. I have spoken and so it is." He teased his tongue along the line of her lower lip. "We've got naught to do today but get it right. And I'm going to try very hard to get it right for you."

There was something about him, a confidence that translated to arrogance, perhaps the innate certainty of a man who operated daily in the role of protector, but Kate found herself letting go of the underlying concern that she might not return home. Never, ever in her life had she done something so decadent with her time as spending the afternoon devoted to carnal pleasure. And now, apparently, she had nothing else to do with her time. She knew she was an overachiever, but she brought the same single-minded determination to this that she brought to everything else. She might not have a lot of experience, but determination and enthusiasm went a long way. And she was feeling very…enthusiastic.

Of course, it was rather mind-boggling that of all the women in the past, present, and future to choose from, this man, who really was rather gorgeous, had apparently zoomed in on her in the cosmic scheme of things. Which was weird, but something of a mega self-confidence booster in the womanly wiles department.

It was as if some unseen force had cut through all the noise in her life and reduced her to her essence—a woman intent on finding her pleasure and bringing pleasure to her man in return.

She caught MacTavish by the hand and led him to the sheepskin on the stone floor before the fireplace. "This looks like a good place to start."

GOOD AND BLUIDY RIGHT he wanted this done thoroughly. He'd ne'er ached for a woman before. Never felt as if he'd trade his soul to the devil for another taste of her lips. Katie Wexford had cast a spell on him and the sooner she was gone, the better. And that definitely meant getting it right, so that no vestige of this hunger remained, extinguishing the lust that coursed through him when she was near. He'd make sure they were both sated before he sent her back to ensure she'd be well and truly gone.

He sank to the sheepskin and drew her down between him and the fire. He was a big man and he didn't want to block the heat and he also wanted to see all of her. There was no shame in admitting she was a mystery to him, so unlike any woman he'd known before.

He lay on his side and admired the play of the flickering fire over her skin, the contrast between pale flesh and shadow. Her shorn hair hugged the line of her scalp and curled about her head. Gold studs adorned her small delicate ears. He noted a prickle of gooseflesh along her arm.

"Are you warm enough?"

"I might have a slight chill." Her eyes gleamed with a teasing light.

She was more relaxed—a good sign. "Ah, could I do something to warm you?"

Was that a blush staining her neck and face or merely a trick of the lighting? "Maybe a few more kisses would work nicely."

Darach didn't think Kate a virgin, she was a bit long in the tooth to have not lain with a man, but he'd wager not many had been before him. Not that she wasn't comely and not that her kisses didn't stir a man to the edge of reason. Nay, there was a distance to Kate Wexford. And now there was a charming awkwardness to her flirtation, as if it wasn't a role she'd worn very often.

"Ah, then 'tis my pleasure to warm you, m'lady." And truly, he could think of nothing he'd like better than to kiss her again, except perhaps bury himself between her sweet thighs…but all in good time.

Bearing his weight on one arm, he leaned over and kissed her. Just as before, heat winnowed through him. With a small moan, she opened her mouth and invited him in with a tentative sweep of her tongue against his lips. She linked her arms around his neck and her touch shivered through him. He kissed her harder, deeper, longer, and still it wasn't enough. He scattered kisses along her jaw, down the length of her neck. With each taste of her, his want grew and pooled thick and heavy between his thighs.

Beneath his lips, her heart raced, the pace matching his own. He traced the upper swell of her breasts and she arched her back with a small moan. He fondled her breast through the material and his rod grew harder still at the press of her nipple against his palm. He eased the material down, baring one full breast with its ripe pouting point. He suckled the tender flesh, relishing the taste of her against his tongue, the brush of her warm woman's softness, her scent. He flicked his tongue against her nipple and she arched up into him.

"MacTavish." She uttered his name in a half moan, half pant. Swirling his tongue around the distended point, he drew her into his mouth and suckled. She made a mewling sound in the back of her throat that threatened to send him up in flames. With an impatient tug at the plaid, she freed her other breast.

"Ah, Katie-love, you have a bonnie set of tits." He lent his attention to the newly freed one, lavishing it with the same care and attention.

Beneath him, Kate laughed, a breathy sound that caught in her throat. "And you've got a bonnie mouth, MacTavish."

"The better to pleasure you."

Her eyes dark with desire, she reached between them and loosened the knot that held the plaid in place. She unwrapped the fabric, leaving herself naked before him, like a gift at Michaelmas.

She fair took his breath. She was even lovelier than the first time he'd seen her naked, mayhap because this time she'd taken her clothes off for him instead of just winding up in his bed. She'd made a conscious decision.

He drank in the sight of her—full, round breasts

tipped with pink crests, plump womanly hips to cradle him, soft curls several shades darker than her hair between her thighs, shapely legs to wrap about his waist.

"Aye, you're a most bonnie lass, Katie-love."

"Thank you, MacTavish. That's a good thing to say to a naked woman."

"'Tis naught but the truth."

"Perhaps you'd like to join me in being naked."

Darach smiled. She'd not need to ask twice.

WHILE MACTAVISH DIVESTED himself of his kilt, Kate reached into her purse and pulled out a condom—not that they were hard to find since Torri had shoved a handful her way. She opened the package and took it out, leaving it on the wrapper between them.

She'd seen him naked before and he was just as impressive now. Thick muscles sculpted his shoulders, arms, and thighs. Dark hair sprinkled his chest and his legs. His penis stood proud among a thatch of equally dark hair. He was primitive power and masculinity and anticipation shivered through her.

He dropped to the sheepskin and reached for her.

"What the bluidy hell is that?" he asked, eyeing the condom.

"It's a condom. Birth control." She recalled the

limerick on the bathhouse wall the summer she'd camped with her best friend's family. Feeling faintly ridiculous and a bit juvenile, she recited it now. It was one way to make a point. "In days of old, when knights were bold and rubbers weren't invented, he placed a sock upon his cock and babies were prevented." She dangled the prophylactic between her thumb and index finger. "I think it's a vast improvement over a sock."

He threw back his head and laughter rumbled through him. "Aye. I ken a sheep's bladder is better than a sock."

Who'd have thought when Torri foisted a handful of condoms on her that she'd be having a safe sex discussion in the eighteenth century? She put the wrapper off to the side.

He seemed a smart man and condoms were fairly straight-forward, but she didn't want to take any chances on misapplication. She stroked his rigid length with one hand and he quivered beneath her touch. "May I?"

"Katie-love if you touch me like that, you can do nearly anything." He lay back, propped on his massive arms, every inch the man in charge and she knew a strictly feminine thrill that she was here with him.

She sheathed him—he was dangerously close to proving that one size didn't fit all—and even that simple act held a carnal pleasure for her. But then this man affected her, turned her on, like no man ever had before. She felt almost drunk with want, all her inhibitions stripped away, as if she'd tossed back a couple of martinis. Her condom duty done, she still lingered to play. Using both hands, she stroked the length of him again and his eyes glittered hotter and brighter. She tested the heavy weight of his sac in her hand and he groaned.

She wanted, no, she craved, intimate knowledge of his body. This wasn't a hunger for a man, any man, it was a hunger for this man. His scent. His taste. The cadence of his breathing.

"Let me get to know you MacTavish."

"Aye, I think I am all for this process, Katie-love." His slow, wicked grin spiked her internal temperature a few degrees.

She spent the next few minutes roaming, discovering his body with her hands and mouth, catching up with where her imagination had taken her over the last several weeks. There was a familiarity to the texture of his skin beneath her lips, the slight saltiness of his body beneath her tongue, a recognition, as if she'd known him for weeks, years, possibly a lifetime and this was simply reality catching up.

She brushed her lips against the puckered skin that stretched from his back to his side, her cheek resting against his hip, her bare breasts against his muscled, hair-roughened thigh.

"Do you know me well enough now, Katie-love?" he asked, his voice low and warm. She looked up past his flat belly and broad chest to his hooded eyes and his face taut with desire. He reminded her of a king. Despite his nakedness, he lay before the fire cloaked in authority and absolute power, a devastatingly sexy combination.

"I know you well enough, MacTavish."

"Then 'tis time for me to know you."

He wrapped his big hands about her waist and pulled her up his body, a slow sensual slide of skin against skin. Her body rejoiced in his corded muscles and hard planes, the supple suede of his skin and the rough slide of masculine hair against her sensitized flesh, the press of his hard cock against her belly and then her thighs as he pulled her up and up, the abrasion of his chest hair against her nipples, the press of his hands at her waist, his scent that seemed to surround her—the scent that aroused her. She lay atop him, a fire of want raging within her.

She tested the silkiness of his hair against her fingertips. His heart beat against her breasts and his belly muscles tensed beneath her thighs at her touch.

"You were sexy in that painting, but you are infinitely sexier in real life."

She obviously said the right thing. In a smooth, sensuous movement he reversed their positions, with her on her back and him on top of her. Warm, soft sheepskin cushioned her backside from the unyielding stone floor while MacTavish's heat engulfed her from above. He trailed a kiss down her chest and flicked his tongue against her tight nipple. The sensation ricocheted through her and intensified the ache between her thighs. She cried out and rocked her hips against him.

MacTavish nudged her thighs apart and a satyric smile curved his mouth. "I'm going to give you what you came here for."

Arrogant sexy bastard. His words and attitude made her hotter still. She reached between them and wrapped her hand around his cock. There was no mistaking the shudder that coursed through him. She'd seen his reaction when Hamish told him she'd come here because MacTavish needed her. Taunting the lion in his cage perhaps wasn't the smartest move, but she'd be damned if he'd make her out to be some twenty-first century desperate who had to go back nearly three hundred years to find a man willing to sleep with her.

She spread her legs wider and guided him to her

wet portal. Her smile mocked his. "And I'm going to give you what *you* summoned me here for…what you *need*."

6

THE DEVIL TAKE IT but he wanted her. Mayhap not her precisely, but some relief. When it came to a tumble, one lass was much the same as another. She'd given him an itch and he'd scratch it. But he was Darach MacTavish, the Laird of Glenagan and he *needed* no woman. Katie was about to discover exactly who needed whom. Hamish wouldn't deliberately lie, but he was subject to err in his facts.

She'd opened her legs and guided him to her. One fractional move of his hips and his rod teased against her. His body tightened in anticipation. "Ah, Katie-love, you are as hot and wet as a summer storm."

Instead of plunging into her, he delved the wet folds of her channel with his tip until her gasp told him he'd found what he sought. Again and again he rubbed his cock against her, until she grasped his arms with her hands, her nails scoring him, and she met his stroking with quick thrusts. Despite her heated response, she kept her face turned toward the fire and her teeth bit down on her lower lip, yet she couldn't quite contain the soft mewling in the back of her throat. Her body tensed and he knew she was on the brink of finding her pleasure. He eased away from her.

She whipped her head around to face him and tried to tug him back to her. "MacTavish…"

Her utterance was a mixture of reproach, entreaty and protest.

Much as he'd like to slip into her wet heat and find the release hovering so close, it was too soon.

"Patience, Katie-love." He swirled his tongue about one perfect nipple and found reward in her sharp intake of breath. He looked up. "Even though we both consider this practice, truth is, neither of us know what will happen once we have lain together. There's no guarantee you will not disappear from my world immediately afterwards."

"Afraid you'll miss me?"

Cheeky lass. "That's yet to be determined. How will I know until you've gone? But if you are gone after one toss, I'll not have you remembering Darach MacTavish as the world's briefest lover." And he'd not have her confused about which one of them had the greater need.

The evil wench laughed at him.

He flicked his tongue against her other nipple and

her laughter ceased. "I want to make sure you find your pleasure."

She propped herself on her elbows and looked at him, quirking one eyebrow. "Maybe there is something to be said for the eighteenth century, because men I know don't share that particular concern. We'd have already been done."

He paused, his cheek resting just above the soft heat of her belly. Despite the fact that she'd appeared out of nowhere and his intent was to promptly send her back, the idea of another man breathing in her scent, tasting her skin, burying himself between her thighs rankled.

He traced the circle where her pink crest met the smooth alabaster globe of her breast. "Then you have obviously bedded the wrong men."

She sighed her pleasure and arched up into his touch, the tip a tight pouting bud. "You're obviously right and obviously my lot has now improved."

"If that's what you are used to, then it definitely has. In my opinion the more you want something, the better it is once you get it."

"Or sometimes you've wanted it so long, so desperately and you've built it up in your mind and then it doesn't live up to expectations. Or maybe you only want it because you think you can't have it."

Foolish woman. Darach never allowed himself

to give consideration to what he couldn't have. That type of thinking left a man weak. "That is simple enough. Know what you want and make sure you get it."

"And do you always get what you want?"

They both knew he wanted her. And they both knew he was going to have her. "Always."

"Because you're the laird of Glenagan."

"Aye. I'm the laird of Glenagan."

"Is this about me finding my pleasure or is it about you being in charge?"

He kissed his way down the slope of her belly, further aroused by her scent, and paused, parting her damp curls with his thumbs. "Mayhap both."

He dipped his head and sampled her tender, honeyed flesh.

KATE SANK BACK into the sheepskin as MacTavish alternately licked and sucked on her clit. Oh. Yes. Every sensation seemed centered between her legs. The swipe of his tongue…the thrust of his nose against her…the brush of his hair against the tops of her thighs…the heat of his fingers against her folds…. He inserted a finger into her as he continued to stroke her nub with his tongue. "Yes." She panted and fisted her hands into the silky wool and pushed against his finger and mouth, desperate for… "More."

"Aye, Katie-love, there is more." He slid another finger in, stretching her, filling her and she moaned her approval. He moved his fingers in and out while he laved her clit. Each stroke of his fingers and tongue knotted her tighter inside until she thought she'd scream with want, until she writhed with the need to come.

MacTavish stopped and looked up the length of her quivering body at her and Kate *knew* what he was all about, knew what *this* was all about. She'd have her pleasure, but she'd pay the price for her earlier taunt. Or not.

She skimmed her hands down her belly and rested her right hand on her mound, within an inch of where he was poised between her thighs.

He retreated, giving her room. His dark smile, brimming with sexual energy, rocked her but she still issued her challenge. "You know I can finish this myself."

"Aye, you could." His voice was a low, sensual croon. "But would that really satisfy you, Katie-love? Is it your touch you crave?" He fingered her and a shudder wracked her. "Is that what you need? Just to finish and be done?"

Kate had two goals, one immediate, one long-term, both self-serving—to come and to get back home. Opting to go solo wasn't going to adequately achieve either. If she was planning to hang around and/or pursue a relationship with this man, they'd definitely have to address his "need" issues but she wasn't on either count so they didn't have to go there. She'd play by his rules.

She rolled from beneath him and onto her knees to face him. It was an incredibly erotic position, with her backside in the air and her breasts hanging heavy and full. The heat of the fire licked along her exposed backside and her slick channel. She arched her back. This must be what a cat in heat felt like—totally driven by the need, the urge to mate with MacTavish. Poor kitty. Nothing less than the length of his cock would satisfy her.

She shook her head and her breasts swayed. "No. It's not my touch I crave—that wouldn't satisfy me at all. That's really not what I need." She looked at him from the top of his head, past his broad shoulders and muscled arms, past his belly to his jutting erection and powerful thighs, letting him see in her eyes what she wanted. She looked at his sheathed cock, and just to make sure there was no mistake, she licked her lips.

"Come here," he said. His commanding tone and hot glittering eyes belied the lazy smile that curled his lips.

Maybe it was because she was in charge all the

time, of everything, that it came as quite a surprise that she didn't want to be in charge in the bedroom. That it was even more of a turn-on to let him take the lead. Still on her hands and knees, she closed the small gap separating them.

"Now tell me what it is you need," he said.

Kate slid one hand beneath the black silk of his hair and cupped the strong column of his neck, pulling him to her. She brushed his lips with hers. "I want you." She slipped her tongue along his lower lip. "I need you."

His mouth captured hers. Bold, demanding, he tested her response and she answered, meeting his tongue with hers. He cupped her breasts in his hands and toyed with them while he kissed her hard. His tongue in her mouth…his fingers tweaking her nipples…on her knees, her legs spread, her sex ready, quivering…she moaned into his mouth.

He released her and got to his knees. "Turn around and face the fire."

Kate turned. She'd never tried it from behind, it had always struck her as somewhat coarse and demeaning. Now it felt elemental and primal and very right. She dropped to her elbows and wriggled her bottom toward him in invitation.

"Oh, lass…" He grasped her hips in his hands and teased each of her cheeks with his thumbs, spreading her wider. The fire heated her face, but his body heat scorched her from behind. He hesitated the tip of his cock at her opening. "You are so wet and hot."

"For you, MacTavish. Only for you."

That seemed to break through his control. In one smooth motion he entered her.

In that instant it was as if everything inside her stilled, a pause that served as a moment of recognition. For an instant she could swear she stopped breathing, her heart stopped beating, that she ceased *being*. She sensed the same sensation in MacTavish and then it was as if they were both swept up in a maelstrom of want and need and being. Every sensation, every thrust, every stroke of him inside her, every brush of his thighs against her, every sensation was more intense, magnified. It was as if each thrust brought her closer to something she both craved and feared. But it didn't matter because her will was no longer her own. She was caught up in something greater than herself that she didn't quite understand but was powerless to stop even if she wanted to, which she didn't.

"Oh, Katie-love…"

"MacTavish…" She hurtled along on an orgasm that took her where she'd never been and then brought her back, marked, changed, a different person. It was as if she'd found a piece of herself she'd never known was missing.

She lay with her eyes closed, feeling MacTavish's weight on top of her, his breath against her hair, the fullness of him still inside her, and panic swamped her.

What if she opened her eyes and found that she'd hurtled forward to the twenty-first century and taken him along with her? That sex could've certainly done it. What if she opened her eyes and she and MacTavish were naked and connected on the museum floor? More horrifying still, what if they were naked and connected in the ER?

It was like one of those bad dreams come true where you find yourself walking naked down the street. Or at least it had the potential to be. But thus far all she heard was the thundering of her own heart and the rasp of MacTavish's breathing.

Kate squinted her eyes open.

It was almost a relief to find herself still in the eighteenth century, in a castle, on her stomach in front of a fire.

MacTavish wrapped his massive arms around her from behind and nuzzled her neck and shoulder. "Katie-love, I'm glad you found your way naked to my bed."

She laughed, but it actually came out as more of

a sigh. "Hmmm. That was definitely worth the trip."
She could definitely use a little more of that before
she returned home.

He withdrew and Kate rolled to her side, the
better to admire his naked form. Even with his
erection at half-mast, he was beautiful.

Admiration turned to dawning horror. Yes. There
was something worse than if she'd transported them,
naked and co-joined, to her work…and she was
looking right at it. She couldn't believe it. Obviously
one size didn't fit all. MacTavish had broken the
condom.

DARACH LOOKED DOWN. *That* wasn't supposed to
happen. "Bluidy hell."

"Oh my God," she said, staring at him as if he
were the devil himself.

"I am not dancing to celebrate, but 'tis not as if
the world's come to an end."

"Not for you maybe. You're not the one who
could've just gotten pregnant…or worse." She put
her hands over her face. "I can't believe the rubber
busted." She dropped her hands and eyed the useless
"condom" still snugged around his rod, but open on
the end. "But it obviously did."

He rolled off the inept device, walked over and
tossed it into the chamber pot. "I have not got the

pox because I have always used a sheep's bladder and they work a sight better than that." He turned to face her. She'd picked up his plaid and was busy wrapping it around her. "I'm no monk, but I have not bedded every lass that looks my way."

"I'm sure they all look—young and old alike." She tied the plaid in place. Backlit by firelight, wrapped in his plaid, head held high, she looked like a Celtic queen.

Her tone obviously meant it an insult, but he'd take it as a compliment.

"'Tis a fair number—" he tried to lighten her mood "—despite my personality. But I've yet to get one with a bairn. As I said, the sheep has stood me well. When are your courses due?"

She shook her head. "I should pay more attention but I'm not sure." She took a deep breath. "It'll be fine. I just panicked for a moment." She tucked her hair behind her ear and he noted, not for the first time, that she possessed lovely, delicate ears. "And I never panic. I'm trained not to panic." She wrapped her arms around her middle and he had the distinct impression she was repeating it so it would be so.

Darach knew a moment of sympathy for her plight. He wouldn't panic—battle taught a man a clear head, else he wound up dead. But he could easily see where she would have lost her head. "'Tis to be expected. You're in a strange place, in a strange time, with a strange man and you've no idea if you can get back."

She shot a look at him that would've withered a lesser man. "Thanks, MacTavish. Now I feel much better. Not to mention I could be pregnant."

There'd been something different when he'd tumbled her—something fey and unfamiliar—she'd touched a part of him that had never been touched before. Now the thought that in that moment they might've created a bairn…."If you were, 'twould definitely be better if you went back."

She eyed him as if he were a bit of offal clinging to her hem. "That would definitely make it more convenient for you, wouldn't it?" She turned her back to him and studied the fire as if it held the answers she sought.

To be sure, something strange had happened tonight for he'd never felt the need to explain himself to a woman before, but he found himself doing just that. "You do not understand. I dunnae ken what it is like in your Atlanta, but I would wager being a MacTavish there wouldnae be nearly as dangerous. And I cannae say it is only the English who would harm a child…or a woman. Many a Scotsman would as well. There is a fair number of men who consider wives and children as weaknesses to be exploited."

"I'm not sure that it's much better where I'm from. We have our share of psychopaths. Not that I want to stay, but surely it's not that bad here."

She had to understand, for her own safety. "You are safe enough here—as long as you stay in here, in this room. That's why I bound you to the bed. 'Twould be madness for you to go out on your own." He could protect her from the men in the castle by declaring her his own. But that brought danger from another source. "And were you carrying my bairn, 'twould not be safe for either you or the child."

He had enemies and he knew they only waited, biding their time, which was one of the reasons he'd never formed an attachment to any woman, why he'd never declared one particular woman his, why he'd made sure never to leave a woman with child. He'd not hand down what might very well be a death sentence.

The tilt of her head, the purse of her lips all bespoke skepticism. "But I saw women and children when I looked out the window."

"They all belong to the clan MacTavish, but none of the bairns are mine, nor are the women." Or they hadn't been until now. Now it was as if she belonged to him, with him, whether he wanted that or not. Even though he lived with a memory, one that haunted his sleep at night. He never spoke of it, but speak he would now and perhaps this stubborn woman would then understand. He grasped her by the shoulders. "I am laird by default. My two older brothers and my mother were all killed by Campbells. They were butchered like swine."

Horror and, more importantly, understanding flickered in her eyes, but she remained calm. "I'm sorry. That must have been horrible. Why? How old were you? How old were they?"

"I was six." It could have been yesterday. Nightmares kept the memory fresh. "My brothers were eight and ten. My mother had lost two bairns after me, but she was pregnant again. 'Twas a fine spring day and we'd spent the morn picnicking at a burn." He could still hear his mother's laughter as "her lads" entertained her with their antics. "Mother said we had to go, but I didn't want to leave. I had a fine time skipping stones across the burn and chores waited at home, so I hid."

For years afterwards, with the reasoning of a child, he'd longed to turn back time. If he'd come when she'd called him, if he hadn't hid, if his mother and brothers hadn't wasted time seeking him, they'd have been gone. They'd have been back and safe at the castle where no Campbell would've dared attack. "While my mother and brothers searched for me, a band of Campbells attacked. They killed them. They searched for me but couldnae find me. I'd hidden well and good and I stayed hidden." He couldn't mask the bitter self-loathing for the role he'd played in their deaths.

She caught his hand in hers and her touch seemed to leech some of the bitterness from his soul. "You were in shock."

"Mayhap I was a coward." Aye, he lived with that every day as well.

Kate shook her head and frowned at him. "You were a child. The only thing you could've done was get yourself killed as well."

"There would've been no danger in that. I saw what they did to Gavin and terror struck me dumb. I crouched in my hiding place and pissed myself while my brother died." 'Twas a shame he'd ne'er shared with anyone. "It would've been better to die trying. I was a coward once, but never again."

"Surely no one blamed you. Surely your father never blamed you."

"Blame me? Nay. He considered it a sign. From that day he considered me the true chosen laird and he trained me as such."

"That sounds ominous."

He'd learned to heft a claymore and broadsword at the same time, one in each hand, a deadly combination and a feat of which few grown men were capable. Every aching muscle, every torturous cramping of muscle had been penance. He shrugged. "'Twas my fate."

"What happened to the men who killed your family?" She asked, but he could see it in her eyes that she already knew.

He nodded in affirmation. "They died. Each of them. 'Twas *their* fate."

"You killed them, didn't you?"

"Aye. 'Twas my duty…and my pleasure. None died quick. I made sure of it." They'd paid for what they'd done to his family. And even though they'd repaid their debt, extracting revenge hadn't lessened his.

"How old were you?"

"Ten. I spent four years in training and planning. Does that frighten you?"

"No. It doesn't frighten me. It disturbs me that you were put in that position. You were a child. What about your father?"

"Aye. He wanted the pleasure of killing them himself, but I begged to do it. 'Twas my debt to pay. And he knew it would prove to the clans my worthiness of being laird even though I was a third son."

She didn't mask her distaste quite fast enough. Aye. How could she, a foreigner, ken the Highland ways?

"Is that how you came by that scar?"

"Aye. 'Twas the first man and I was not quite fast enough. Da made sure I got faster after that."

"What about your father? Is he still alive?"

"He died a few years ago. Nothing bloody. He just went to sleep and never woke up." She might not ken their ways, but he'd wager she understood the importance of not leaving this room and why no bairn of his belonged at Glenagan. "And you understand now?"

"Yes. I understand. The odds are that I'm not pregnant, but either way I'm going to do everything I can to figure out how to get myself home. And when I get there, if I'm pregnant, I'll do everything in my power to make sure nothing like that ever happens to my child."

His child. Their child. It left him with a distinctly odd feeling.

7

MAYBE MACTAVISH WASN'T such an arrogant bastard after all. He stood before her—naked yet commanding, with his broad shoulders and heavily muscled arms, legs like strong trees, flowing black hair, and chiseled harsh features saved by a sensual mouth. Forget it. He was still arrogant, but now she understood life's harsh lessons that had shaped him.

A knock sounded on the heavy wooden door. Kate jumped, nearly clearing the floor. It had been far too easy to forget they weren't the only two human beings on earth.

"Your food." A man's voice—Hamish?—called from the other side.

Without regard for his naked state, MacTavish strode across the room. Uncertain as to who stood on the other side and still cautious after hearing his horrifying story—not to mention the fact that she was in that same harsh place in that same lawless time—Kate took cover in the deep shadows on the other side of the fire. Away from the heat, the chill of the stone floor bit into her bare feet. She fisted her hands in the wool she wore and shivered in the draft that seemed worse in this corner of the room.

MacTavish threw open the door. Relief flooded her when she recognized Hamish's prematurely grey head. He carried a laden wooden tray. "Is she still here?"

Kate stepped forward. "Yes."

MacTavish nodded his head toward the room, motioning Hamish inside. "Come in."

Hamish did as MacTavish instructed. He crossed the room and placed the tray on the table next to her breakfast bowl. MacTavish closed the door.

Raking his hands through his hair, MacTavish turned to Hamish. "Can you give us no clue? No information as to why she's here and how she can get back?"

He shook his white head in wordless apology. "Would that I could be more helpful. But I dunnae ken any more than I have told. I am a go-between."

"A conductor?" Kate recalled her first impression of Hamish at the museum.

"Aye, mayhap a conductor. I recognize you, but I dinnae know you. I know about my life in the timeframe you are from. I know I exist there." He caught MacTavish's eye. "'Twas the two of you what brought her here. 'Twill be the two of you that send the lass back. 'Tis a puzzle you'll need to solve."

MacTavish's mouth drew a grim line across his face, leaving it harsh indeed.

Her conversation with Hamish in the museum hit her like a gale-force wind. How could she have forgotten something so terrible, so important? In her defense, the experience had been disconcerting to say the least and she'd been focused on herself and returning to Atlanta and the twenty-first century.

She'd much prefer Hamish bear the bad news. Maybe she could jog his memory. "Don't you recall the conversation we had in front of the painting last night before I came here?" Put that way, it sounded as if she'd taken a brief taxi ride.

"Nay. You are familiar but while I know of this time when I am in your time, that's because it is the past. But when I'm in the past, such as now, I can't know of then because it has not happened for me yet. Bits and pieces hover in the back of my mind, much like a dream you can't quite recall."

Great. It was up to her. How many times had she handed down a preliminary diagnosis from which a patient would never recover? How many times had she faced a family to tell them their loved one was lost, that the ER staff hadn't been able to save them, whether it had been to a gunshot wound or a heart attack or a stroke? Countless. She handed down death sentences on a far more regular basis than she liked. She sought the calm professionalism, the training that saw her through those moments, but couldn't seem to find it. Her stomach roiled even as she squared her shoulders and faced the man she'd just enjoyed incredible sex with. There was no sugarcoating it and he struck her as a man who'd take his bad news straight up.

She looked MacTavish in the eye. "You die in the spring of 1745 on the battlefield at a place called Drumossie Moor."

Other than sharing a brief glance with Hamish, his countenance didn't change, yet a sudden tension filled the room. "How do you know this?"

She nodded toward Hamish. "He told me. History's not my thing so it was all news to me. He said you were the last MacTavish laird. You died without a wife or a child. And the men—" she looked toward Hamish "—I think you called them Jacobites—"

"Aye. We be Jacobites."

Kate continued, "The men that didn't die on the battlefield were hunted down and killed." Unlike discussing a fatal disease or condition with a patient, calmly putting forth the facts of MacTavish's impending demise chilled her. She shivered. "I'm sorry."

MacTavish paced to the fire and stared into the flames, not acknowledging her last comment. A dark silence filled the room's space. Finally he turned his back to the fire and faced her. "Did he tell you anything else? Think hard. Recount every detail. What may seem unimportant to you may mean something to us."

Kate once again repeated what she knew in the hopes that an overlooked fact would spill forth. She couldn't have made this journey in time simply to tell a man he and his people would soon perish. "He said you were the last laird of the clan MacTavish. You and your clansmen died on the battlefield and that was the end of not just your clan but all the Highland clans. You were all there because you wanted to restore Bonnie Prince Charlie to the throne."

"If the clans ended with that battle, 'tis apparent he never gained the throne. Was Drumossie Moor the destination that day or were we intercepted by the Sassenach there?"

Frustration gnawed at her that she couldn't shed more light on the situation. "I don't know." She glanced to the man who was the link between past and present. "Hamish didn't say and I'd never heard of the Battle of Culloden."

"You said Drumossie Moor." His tone rang sharp, that of an interrogator.

She was beginning to feel like a criminal under investigation when she'd done nothing other than show up at the wrong time in the wrong place. Her response cut equally sharp. "Yes, it was Drumossie and it later became known as Culloden."

Hamish knotted his hands together. "Did I give you any specific dates?"

"No. I'd definitely remember if you'd mentioned a specific date—my memory is excellent with numbers."

Hamish sighed and rubbed his hand over his face. "Then we have only a general time frame, a place and a dour outcome."

MacTavish crossed to the window she'd looked out of earlier. "This is bluidy bonnie. I've got a bit of information I can do naught with." He turned his back to the window, frustration etched in his face, in the set of his shoulders. "Am I to go to the other clans and announce we will all die sometime in the spring? They will think me daft or a traitor, or mayhap both." He turned to Hamish, "But I ken we have our answer as to why she's here."

Okay, she took back any qualifiers she might have made about him not being an arrogant jerk. She hadn't exactly dropped good news in their laps, but she wasn't standing for this. "I'd prefer to not be spoken of and ignored as if I'm not in the room."

MacTavish didn't spare her a glance. "Even though she didnae give us anything we could really use."

Enough. The stress, the uncertainty, the emotional roller coaster that had been the last eighteen hours came to a head. She planted herself in front of him, despite the fact that he could snap her like a twig if he chose to.

"Listen, Darach MacTavish, laird of Glenagan, I didn't ask to come here." She poked the hard wall of his chest to make sure she got his attention. "I don't want to be here." She poked again for emphasis. "And I'm sorry I didn't have better news to tell you, but there's no need to shoot the messenger." She threw in a third poke for good measure.

He crossed his massive arms across his massive chest, presumably to preclude future poking, and stared hard down his harsh nose at her.

Maybe that look worked on his subjects or whatever his people were called, but it only further infuriated her. "What? You think this is a party for me? I go from a very respected, well-paid job as a doctor and a very nice condo to this." She waved her arm around the room. "No electricity. No running water. No flush toilets. No Starbucks. No cell phone. No sleep number beds."

She threw up her hands in disgust. "I might as well be speaking a foreign language because none of that means jack to you because you don't have any of it in this godforsaken land in this godforsaken year. So, I go from that to this and to top it off the rubber broke and now I might be knocked up with the baby of the original dead man walking. If anyone's got a right to be pissed off it's me. And one more thing, while we're getting the facts straight, I'm not part of your problem. And if I'm not part of your problem then it stands to reason that I'm part of your solution, so Mr. High and Mighty Laird of Glenagan perhaps you should start treating me with some respect. I'm a smart woman and if you were a smart man you'd take advantage of my brains instead of simply my body."

He opened his mouth to speak and she cut him off. She wasn't through. "And one more thing. I would've gone home and Googled the Battle of Culloden and had all kinds of nifty factoids for you if he'd—" she stabbed a finger in Hamish's direction "—given me a chance. But no, five minutes after he tells me your story, he's shoving me into the painting. It wasn't as if I had an opportunity to do anything with the information other than show up and tell you what little I know."

Hamish, wearing a sheepish expression, shrugged. "I have no answer except that if the timing had not been right you wouldnae have made the journey. Ye would have banged into the painting, bounced off the wall, thought me a daft old man and been on your merry way. But I ken you just said you might be with a bairn." He developed a sudden interest in his nails. "Mayhap that is why you are here."

Kate had only thought herself chilled before. That thought froze her—alone and pregnant in a foreign land in a foreign century with no skill to support herself and her child. She shifted closer to the fire. "No."

"'Tis logical you would be here to provide a MacTavish heir," Hamish said. His demeanor and soothing even voice reminded her of a clergyman.

She stood straighter. "I am not a brood mare." Her statement would've had more impact had she not been clothed in MacTavish's kilt with his scent still clinging to her skin and her body still pleasantly achy from his recent possession.

"Mayhap 'tis Darach's destiny to die on the battlefield, yet the MacTavish line need not die with him."

"Hel-lo? I said no. No, no, and no. I don't want to have a baby. And I sure don't want to have *his* baby." She looked over at where Darach stood glowering at them both. "Nope. I know all about genetics. Wouldn't I love to have a kid with *that* temperament? Perish the thought." She crossed her arms beneath her breasts. Dammit but it galled her to stand around wrapped in MacTavish's kilt. She felt branded by it. But it was better than striding about naked the way the arrogant Laird of Glenagan seemed to favor.

"Sometimes it matters not what we want. Sometimes there are greater forces at work than our wills," Hamish said. This guy was seriously working her nerves. "How often have you experienced…how did you put it, the rubber breaking?"

Damn Hamish's sly reasoning. "Never before." Please. No. "Listen, I am so sure one of the women here in the castle is a much better candidate for this than me. They can provide a good genetic match and they're familiar with the time and place. If it's an heir you want, you really should choose one of them."

"But none of them traveled through time to get here—"

"No!" MacTavish exploded, banging his fist on the table and rattling the tray's contents. "I want no heir and I want no mother of my child." He glared at Hamish and Kate knew a moment of trepidation. In a temper, MacTavish was truly formidable. A peculiar expression shadowed his eyes. "Especially not if I am tae die and willnae be here to protect them."

Finally. They were getting somewhere. Kate looked at Hamish. "See, he's on my side. He doesn't want me or a baby and I don't want him or a baby. That should count for something. It's two to one."

Hamish smiled and shook his head. "I am just about solving the puzzle of your being here and how to get you back."

Kate felt better. It wasn't as if he had an inside track or knew something they didn't. He was just speculating and throwing out ideas. "We call that brainstorming. Brainstorming's good." She turned to MacTavish. "Okay. Let's look at the other possibilities. Perhaps you don't have to die."

"I will nae live again as a coward."

She looked to Hamish, hoping for some guidelines. "Can history be re-written? Can a course of events be changed?"

"Aye. If it is meant to be. I think yer both forgetting an important piece of this puzzle. There is destiny, which is a greater plan beyond our control, and there is free will and often we do not know which is which. We do not know what we can change and what we can not. So, it may matter not what either of you think you want."

Kate impatiently shoved a curl behind her ear. "But you said it was both of our wants—" she shot

MacTavish a hard glance, he owned this as much as she did, actually more in her opinion "—our needs, that brought me here. So apparently our wants do matter."

Hamish acknowledged her reasoning with a reluctant nod. "It would seem so, but mayhap only if in keeping with your destiny. 'Tis an enigma only the two of you can discern. Your connection was through a Sex Through the Ages exhibit." He glanced at Kate in apology. "Begging your pardon for speaking blunt but mayhap 'tis nothing more than you shagging him 'til he dies." He shook his head and grinned. "Hardly seems fair. If Darach is to die at Drumossie, then 'tis likely my fate as well. Couldnae you have brought along a friend fer me?"

MacTavish laughed and Kate stared at both men, confounded. One minute they were embroiled in a serious discussion of destiny and their impending demise and the next they were laughing like schoolboys. "If I'd only known…"

MacTavish seemed to know exactly what she was thinking. "Daft Scot and his gallows humor."

"Very few people laugh when they find out they're going to die soon," she said.

"I am not afraid tae die." MacTavish shrugged. "I've waited a long time for death. But I cannae sit by and do nothing for my people. I cannae leave the women to be raped and worse and the men to be hunted and killed by the English dogs."

Kate shuddered at the scene he painted, the scene due to play out all too soon. "Then we don't have a choice. We have to keep working on it until we come up with a solution."

MacTavish rocked back on his heels. "There is a possibility we have all overlooked."

"Yes?" Kate said.

"Speak up, man," Hamish said.

"A few minutes ago you said if Hamish had not sent you through the painting so quick you would have had more facts for me. You also said you were not of the problem, you were of the solution. Mayhap, there lies our answer. No answers lie here, only questions and uncertainty. All the answers belong in your time. Hamish was right after all. I do *need* you. You need to take me back with you, Katie-love."

Hamish nodded. "Bluidy brilliant."

MacTavish turned his dark eyes on her. "But I will wager I can only come if you want me. Do you want me, Katie-love?" His gaze pierced her very soul.

Her heart thumped so loudly, surely he could hear it from where he stood. "You're arrogant and bossy and ill-tempered, MacTavish." He had only asked her to take him for a short period of time—

long enough for him to gather facts and devise a plan. Why then, did it feel as if she was about to utter an eternal vow? "Aye, I want you."

8

KATE CLUTCHED HER PURSE and paced across the room, almost giddy with excitement at their impending journey. Once again, she wore the MacTavish plaid. MacTavish had finally donned one himself. She stifled a laugh at the thought that they looked like a couple doing the matching outfits thing—only to the extreme. "Are you ready for the twenty-first century?"

She wasn't sure what she looked forward to the most—the comfort of a modern bathroom, a good cup of coffee, or the advantages of modern technology such as her pager actually working.

"There is no guarantee this will work," MacTavish warned her as he pulled on his boots.

"It will. I've always been very practical and fact-oriented and this is neither…but since I saw the painting that first time, it was as if something awakened in me. I don't quite know how to describe it—a sixth sense maybe, a latent intuition. And since I've been here, it's grown stronger and stronger."

She held up her hands in a questioning gesture. "Maybe because facts as I know them no longer make sense. From a factual standpoint, I shouldn't have been able to walk into a picture and travel back more than two-hundred sixty years in time."

"'Tis a strange thing to be sure." He stood and Kate silently admired the figure he cut in his kilt and boots.

"It's beyond strange. But I have a sense that this is right—you're supposed to go with me—and this is how we're supposed to do it." She hadn't been so sure until they'd made love the second time. Now she knew with absolute certainty.

"You are ready to go home, are you not, Katie-love?"

"I can't wait."

"Aye. You made it very clear that this—" he swept his hand toward the room "—does not compare to your home."

Oops. She'd definitely wounded his pride with her earlier comments. It really wasn't like her at all to fly off the handle. "I'm sorry I said those things. I was angry. The main thing is I don't belong here. This isn't my home and these aren't my people."

She was a total fish out of water with no chance of adapting to this place and time.

"No. You do not belong here." His dark eyes held hers. "'Tis definitely time for you to go home."

"Where I'm from is wonderful. Just wait, Mac-Tavish. You won't believe it." It almost bordered on cruelty to give him a taste of the good life only to send him back to this land of hardship and deprivation. But this had a rightness to it and they'd each do what they had to do. "The hardest part will be getting you to my condo. Then we're home free. I'm nervous, though, as to where we'll show up and how we'll be dressed—make that *if* we'll be dressed. I assure you I wasn't wandering the museum naked but that's how I showed up here." She glanced at the picture on the wall beside her.

MacTavish offered a wicked grin. "Aye. And twas a pleasure to behold."

Men. She shook her head at him. "Thank you. But it'll be better if we have on clothes when we get there. The most important thing, and I know this won't be easy for you, is you've got to do what I tell you to do. I know you're accustomed to being in charge, but let me do the talking and follow my lead."

"'Tis true I am used to being in charge." He crossed his arms over his chest. "But I will do as you say…as long as I agree with what you tell me to do."

"That's not the way it works. You might not particularly understand why I'm saying something or doing something. You know, I wasn't crazy about being locked in this room. But you told me to stay and I stayed."

He leveled a glance that immediately brought to mind her meeting him in the circular stairwell.

"Okay. Except for that one time. But it's like here." She waved a hand around the room. "You can't tell anyone you're almost three hundred years old. People will think you're crazy. And if they think you're crazy and dangerous…well, they'll lock you up." Simply thinking of the psych ward sent a shiver through her. "And you don't want to be locked up. It's not a good place to be and it's not going to help you help your people. I need your word on this, MacTavish."

He stood with his feet planted apart, a stubborn cast to his jaw.

"You've got to trust me. I'm just trying to help you. But I can't if you won't let me. So, even though it might seem that I'm in charge, you're ultimately in charge."

The glower in his eyes turned to a glimmer of amusement. He shook his head at her doubletalk. "You have my word. I'll do as you say."

She knew that hadn't come easy for him. "Thank you. This shouldn't be that difficult if you keep sort of quiet. Atlanta's a big city and there are people there from all over the world so, as long as you're not naked and if we can get you in some regular clothes, no one will notice, MacTavish."

"I have a suggestion tae make…before you are in charge."

"Yes?"

"Mayhap you should call me by my given name."

She knew that. She really did. It was irrational, and as a rule she was never irrational, but even though she'd slept in his bed, worn his clothes, eaten his food, and made love with him, there was an intimacy and familiarity in calling him by his first name that she'd avoided. "You're right. I'll make sure I do."

"Do it now, so that you get used to it," he said.

She could swear he knew how reluctant she was and why. Fine. "Darach."

Dammit. She knew it. Even though she'd been matter-of-fact, it felt intimate. MacTavish kept him at a distance. MacTavish was larger than life, the laird of Glenagan. But Darach… Darach was just a man.

An expression she could almost mistake for tenderness chased across his face and vanished. "I know you're very sure we will both travel to your Atlanta. I cannae say I feel as sure. And if that's the case, I cannae let you go without saying good bye." He stroked the backs of his fingers along her face.

"'Tis been a pleasure to know you, Katie Wexford. Godspeed to you." He splayed his hands intimately across her belly. "And if mayhap, you are carrying my bairn, be it lad or lassie, will you give it the MacTavish name and one day tell it of me?"

Despite the fact that she had found him infuriating on more than one occasion, the unexpected pain of his goodbye nearly tore her asunder, as if a limb was being ripped from her body. "Yes. You have my word. If there's a baby, it will carry the MacTavish name." It almost made her wish…. No.

"My mother's name was Isobel. 'Tis a bonnie name for a lass."

She caught a glimpse of the boy he must've been before circumstances and time had molded him, hardened him. Tears burned behind her eyes and she had to swallow hard before she could speak. "Isobel is a lovely name."

Obviously she hadn't swallowed hard enough because a tear trickled down her cheek. She brushed it away impatiently. She would not leave him behind to die at Drumossie.

"I'm not saying goodbye because you're coming with me," she said. "I need you so that we can figure this out. This can't be the way it was meant to end. I need you. Come with me, Darach."

She linked her arms around his neck and kissed

him. She poured herself into the kiss, into him—her soul, her mind, her body. He bore her back against the wall and it was more than a mere fusing of mouths and tongues. It was a fusing of souls and wills that transcended the physical. Locked together in a kiss she felt herself spiraling, tumbling, whirling in the dark as she'd done once before.

Darach broke the kiss and rested his forehead against hers. "Katie-love…" He sounded as dizzy and disoriented as she still felt.

Kate blinked her eyes open, adjusting to the dim lighting. She and Darach were leaning against the museum wall, next to the painting, near the exact spot she'd stood to admire the portrait before Hamish had shoved her. "Look. Look around us." They'd done it without really trying. They'd done it! Together, they'd traveled through time.

"Welcome to Atlanta and the twenty-first century, Darach MacTavish."

WHAT HAD HE EXPECTED the journey to be like? Perhaps the wind rushing by him? Perhaps he'd soar through the air like a hawk, an Icarus, with majestic sweeping views of the Highland wilds below him?

He for certain hadn't expected to spin so out of control that he almost lost consciousness.

Darach looked about him. Various portraits hung

about on smooth plaster walls that soared high. Some lamps with no torch or candle actually burning. Gleaming wood floors. Aye, 'twas a strange place.

"Glad to see you made it here." He turned and found himself face to face with a man who appeared to be a much older version of Hamish by thirty or forty years.

"Hamish?"

"One and the same." He grinned and Darach for sure recognized his friend. "Good trip?"

"Aye. 'Twas a bit rough but it happened in not much more than the blink of an eye."

Hamish cast a concerned eye on Kate and Darach. "Time travel affects everyone differently. It leaves some feeling a bit sickish. You two okay?"

Kate nodded, her face wreathed in a smile that reminded him of a glimpse of the sun following a storm. "I've never felt better." She turned to Darach. "How about you?"

Well, truth be told he had been better because 'twas all strange and even Hamish sounded different. But, he'd made it and at least now he had a glimmer of hope that he could save his people. "Aye. I'm fine."

Hamish passed a change of clothes to Darach. "I thought you might show up and I figured you'd need this. You'll blend in much better without the plaid.

Quick. Change here. There's no one around but you'll want to hurry, the museum's just closing now."

Darach looked at the garments in his hand.

Hamish nodded toward the room's open doorway. "I'll keep an eye out while you dress. Perhaps your lady can give you a hand, since it's a bit different from what you're used to."

Kate. He'd been so busy taking it all in, he hadn't noticed until now that she wore trousers and a shirt with a jacket. He preferred her naked or wrapped in his kilt. Or mayhap it was because he'd just left a bit of himself with her in that kiss and now she looked more a stranger than the woman he'd come to know.

She plucked a white undergarment from the top and presented it to him.

Darach briefly examined it before he handed it back.

"Nay. Scotsmen dinnae wear those. 'Tis a matter of pride."

Katie planted a hand on her hip. Different century and country or not, that must be a universal lass gesture. "Are you suffering short-term memory loss? We just talked about this. You know—that discussion where you agreed to do what I say without arguing. When we get to my house, you can take them off and turn your big boy loose, but until then, put them on."

An Important Message from the Editors

Dear Reader,

Because you've chosen to read one of our fine novels, we'd like to say "thank you"! And, as a special way to thank you, we're offering you a choice of two more of the books you love so well, and a surprise gift to send you – absolutely FREE!

Please enjoy them with our compliments...

Pam Powers

Peel off Seal and
Place Inside...

FREE GIFT SEAL
EDITOR'S THANK YOU

THE EDITOR'S "THANK YOU" FREE GIFTS INCLUDE:

- ▶ 2 Romance OR 2 Suspense books
- ▶ An exciting surprise gift

YES! I have placed my Editor's "thank you" Free Gifts seal in the space provided at right. Please send me the 2 FREE books which I have selected, and my FREE Mystery Gift. I understand that I am under no obligation to purchase anything further, as explained on the back of this card.

PLACE
FREE GIFTS
SEAL
HERE

Check one:

ROMANCE
193 MDL EE39   393 MDL EE4M

SUSPENSE
192 MDL EE4L   392 MDL EE4X

FIRST NAME

LAST NAME

ADDRESS

APT.#

CITY

STATE/PROV.

ZIP/POSTAL CODE

(ED1-HON-06) © 1998 MIRA BOOKS

The Reader Service — Here's How It Works:

Accepting your 2 free books and gift places you under no obligation to buy anything. You may keep the books and gift and return the shipping statement marked "cancel." If you do not cancel, about a month later we'll send you 3 additional books and bill you just $5.24 each in the U.S., or $5.74 each in Canada, plus 25¢ shipping & handling per book and applicable taxes if any.* That's the complete price and — compared to cover prices starting from $5.99 each in the U.S. and $6.99 each in Canada — it's quite a bargain! You may cancel at any time, but if you choose to continue, every month we'll send you 3 more books, which you may either purchase at the discount price or return to us and cancel your subscription.

*Terms and prices subject to change without notice. Sales tax applicable in N.Y. Canadian residents will be charged applicable provincial taxes and GST.

If offer card is missing write to: The Reader Service, 3010 Walden Ave., P.O. Box 1867, Buffalo, NY 14240-1867

BUSINESS REPLY MAIL
FIRST-CLASS MAIL   PERMIT NO. 717-003   BUFFALO, NY

POSTAGE WILL BE PAID BY ADDRESSEE

THE READER SERVICE
3010 WALDEN AVE
PO BOX 1341
BUFFALO NY 14240-8571

NO POSTAGE
NECESSARY
IF MAILED
IN THE
UNITED STATES

He wasn't taken in by her sweet smile. Damn the wretched woman, but she was enjoying this.

He stepped into the underwear and pulled them up. "Bluidy hell. How can a man think with his rod all bundled up next to his sack?"

"Don't whine, Darach. Take off the kilt and put on this shirt." While he took off his kilt and shrugged into the shirt, she examined the jacket and turned to Hamish. "Versace? Did you pick this out?"

Hamish, from his lookout, nodded and offered a sheepish grin. "Aye. Since I've been in the twenty-first century, I've discovered I like shopping. The shopping network is addictive."

"You bought a Versace suit on the shopping network?" she asked.

Hamish laughed. "Neiman's was having a sale and I couldn't help myself. I kept the receipt in case he didn't show up."

They might as well have been speaking a foreign tongue, Darach thought, because he dinnae ken Versace, the shopping network, or Neiman's, but he knew fer damn sure he preferred his kilt to this. And while Hamish looked the same, except a good bit older, he dinnae know this man the way he knew the Hamish of old—the Hamish of his boyhood. This Hamish owned a worldliness that was at odds with the man Darach knew—neither good nor bad, just different.

He finished dressing while Kate and Hamish talked.

"Where do I store my kilt and boots?" he asked.

Hamish crossed to a small table displaying dildoes. He reached beneath the cloth draping it and pulled out a black-handled leather satchel.

"This should hold them," he said as he passed Darach the satchel.

Katie looked at him, the heat in her eyes almost worth the discomfort of the clothes he wore. But mayhap he also knew a moment of disappointment that she seemed to like this better than his plaid, which was as much a part of who and what he was as the blood that flowed through his veins.

"Oh. My. I'm going to have to beat the women off with a stick." She looked to Hamish. "He might as well have worn the kilt. He's going to be noticed regardless of what he wears."

If that was the case…."I will be glad tae change."

"No. You will actually fit in better this way—" another look that stirred his blood "—but certainly no one's going to overlook you." Kate glanced at her wrist and then looked once more. "My watch is working again. What day is it?" she asked Hamish. "What time is it?"

"It's the same day, same time it was when you left. Because you spent your time in the past, you lost no time here. The future had yet to exist. But it doesn't work that way when you come from the past. The sand is still sifting through the hourglass at Glenagan just as it is here now." He nudged Darach and gestured to the painting behind him. "It's weathered the years well, don't you think?"

For the first time Darach looked at the painting. "'Tis the same, just a bit older."

Hamish nodded. "This is how Kate got to you and this is how you'll return to Glenagan. As you know, the exhibit is now closed here. After tonight, it's officially in transit. It reopens in New York in two weeks and will be there for two months. Before I leave, I'll secure a passport for you to make sure there's no trouble flying to New York. We'll get a photo taken in a couple of days. Once there, you have but to find the portrait when you're ready to return." He clapped his arm about Darach's shoulder, enveloping him in a hug. "Good luck, Darach."

"How do we contact you if we need to in the next two weeks?" Kate asked. She didn't want to know how he was going to secure what would clearly be an illegal passport.

He reached into his vest pocket and pulled out a pen and paper. "If you have any questions—or if you just want to do lunch—" he jotted down a number and handed it to her "—give me a call on my cell."

2

"GOOD NIGHT." The same blazer-clad attendant who'd merely given her a cursory glance on the way in, was now all smiles and checking Darach out. Not surprising.

Hamish definitely had an eye for clothes. Mac-Tavish was drop-dead gorgeous in a kilt—and she had first-hand knowledge that he was equally drop-dead gorgeous in the buff—but this suit.... The trousers and jacket were a fine wool/cashmere blend that hung from his broad shoulders and lean hips as if it had been custom-made to showcase his body. A black collared shirt, top button left open, completed the outfit. His long black hair hung past his shoulders and framed the masculine beauty of his face with his hooded eyes, harsh nose, and sensual mouth.

By rights, Darach should have been just another person in a city of thousands. In 1744, at Glenagan, he was laird with absolute power. But obviously his arrogance, surety, power came from within because even in a vastly different time and place, he still exuded power, intelligence, fearlessness and sex appeal—a dark, dangerous man to reckon with and sexy beyond reason.

Small wonder the museum attendant couldn't keep her eyes off of him. Kate bid the woman good-night and pushed through the glass doors with Darach right behind her.

They stepped out into Atlanta's warm autumn evening. The door closed behind them and Kate stopped to give Darach a moment to take it all in and get his bearings. Leaves, kicked up by a wind carrying a hint of chill, danced about their feet. Traffic flowed along Peachtree Street, a cacophony of sound—the muted blare of rap played too loud, the intermittent honk of horns, the rumble of cars, and the voices of pedestrians. The city, the resplendent melting pot of the south, lay before them.

"This is Atlanta, Georgia," she said. What would he think of her world and the city she'd adopted as her own in the last few years? Butterflies fluttered in her stomach and she realized she was nervous which was altogether silly. It didn't matter what he thought of her world any more than her opinion of his. She had been sent to give him a heads-up. He was here seeking a solution. End of story. It was amazing their paths had crossed in the vastness of time. But that's all it was, a brief encounter outside time's continuum as she knew it, as the world knew it. She needed to bear that in mind.

For a full minute he scanned the horizon, his gaze sharp, and she knew he missed nothing from the hi-rises to the couple hand-holding at the museum's courtyard fountain to their left. "It has a strange beauty. I've been to Edinburgh before, but much here is beyond my ken."

Kate thought back to when she'd looked out of the castle window at the small village and then the moor that seemed to stretch for miles beyond. She recalled how she'd felt and saw her city through his eyes and his perspective. "It's amazing isn't it?"

"Aye. Even though I don't understand all that I see, 'tis amazing indeed." He turned to her and it was as if a laser had pinpointed her. He had an intensity about him, an energy. He'd dismissed the city and focused now on her. Despite the wind-borne chill, a flush spread through her. "And 'tis amazing I'm here. Thank you, Katie-love, for coming to get me." He caught her hand up in his, his touch tingling through her. "Thank you for giving me the chance to save my people—for bringing me back with you."

He turned her hands in his and brought them to his mouth. He pressed a warm kiss to the blue vein in her wrist, his lips lingering on her pulse point as if he were paying homage to the beat of her heart, to the life force flowing through her. Kate's breath caught in her throat and time seemed to hang suspended, wrapping them in an intimacy. He raised his head and the air chilled her skin in the absence of his warmth.

"My pleasure, Darach MacTavish."

The heat in his hooded eyes told her he felt the same sexual tug. "Aye. And your pleasure is my pleasure. How far to your home from here?"

His husky tone left her pulse racing and her body humming a response. Yes, they had a mission and this was all new and different to him, but they also had two weeks to come up with a solution. Thus far today, they'd made tremendous progress. She was here and he was here. And now she'd like to take him home and get him out of that suit. She wanted to feel him hot and hard inside her again.

"My car's at the hospital—about a twenty-minute walk. It's another ten minute drive to my place."

The wind shifted his hair against his collar. "Take me to your home, Katie." The look in his eyes said he wanted the same thing she did.

The walk passed quickly. Along the way Kate explained the technology that formed the backdrop for her world—automobiles, electricity, cell phones, mass transit. Darach, a quick study, asked intelligent, thoughtful questions. Below the surface of their very urbane discussion, the fire of want and need burned between them, licked at them with flames of desire.

Although he looked at everything with a genuine interest, he seemed oblivious to the myriad female heads he turned. They didn't pass a woman, young or old, who didn't look twice at him. A few even stopped and gawked, but they all noticed.

It reminded her of a demonstration her fourth grade teacher, Mrs. Fitzroy, had performed in elementary school. Mrs. Fitzroy had scattered metal filings all over a table. Then she'd dragged a large magnet down the table's center. All the filings had skimmed across the surface, drawn by the force of the magnet. The magnet, however, had not been impacted at all by the clinging filings.

She wouldn't lie to herself. It was heady stuff that he didn't even blink an eye of interest in their direction. All of his energy, all of his attention remained centered on her.

They stood at the corner, part of a crowd, waiting on the traffic light to change. Ahead of them, a couple stood, arms twined about each other's waist. Darach slipped his arm about her waist, leaned down and murmured in her ear, "I dunnae want to lose you in the crush."

She slid her arm around him, beneath the edge of his jacket, welcoming his heat and the play of muscle beneath his shirt. "And here I thought you just wanted to touch me."

He leaned down, his breath gusting warm against her ear. "Aye. I want to touch you. And when we get to your house, I'll show you…."

Maybe she was giddy at having managed to get back home and bring him with her. Perhaps it was the sexual energy flowing between them. But, on impulse, she slid her hand down his waist, over his backside and grabbed his left cheek. He started in surprise. She smiled up at him and widened her eyes in faux innocence. "Sorry, I couldn't help myself."

"Wench." His eyes glinted with a volatile combination of laughter and sexual heat. She'd try not to get a speeding ticket getting them to her condo.

The light changed and they crossed the street, dodging a workboot on the other corner that someone had obviously lost. MacTavish looked at her, one eyebrow raised in question. She shook her head and laughed. "I have no idea."

They were half a block from the hospital and Kate was about to point out where she worked when someone hailed her from behind.

"Kate? Dr. Wexford?"

She fully intended to pretend she simply hadn't heard but MacTavish ruined that plan by coming to a dead halt, stopping her with him. "Someone's calling for you."

Peachy. She knew. And she knew who—she'd recognized the voice. And she'd prefer dental drilling without the benefit of novocaine over stopping to talk, but MacTavish had left her with no option. She played stupid.

"Oh? Really?" She looked over her shoulder just as Torri bore down on them, her predatory gleam devouring Darach.

"Hello, Dr. Campbell," Kate said.

Torri tossed her long blonde hair over one shoulder, a look-at-me seductive move Kate had seen her employ hundreds of times. "It was you. I was standing in the back, waiting on the light and I thought it was you, but I wasn't certain."

Kate saw it in Torri's surprised expression. Of all people, Torri had seen her grab Darach's ass. Good.

"It's me."

More hair tossing and a lip moué to go with it this time. Torri was pulling out all the stops. "So, this is your hot date?" She looked Darach up and down like a hungry dog eyeing a juicy bone. "I can see why you were so eager to end your shift."

Bitch! Not only was she laying him naked on his back with her eyes, Torri made it sound as if Kate had shunned her duty and run out of the hospital when in actuality she'd stayed two hours after her shift had officially ended. If she pointed that out then she, Kate, would be the one who came off looking bitchy—it was simply one of those injustices in life. And while she might've pretended she didn't hear Torri, she couldn't not offer the introduction Torri was angling for so blatantly.

"Torri, this is, Darach MacTavish. Darach, Dr. Torri Campbell."

With the overnight bag Hamish had provided in his left hand, Darach had to take his arm from around Kate to shake Torri's hand. Yet one more reason to dislike her.

"'Tis a pleasure to meet you, Dr. Campbell." His mouth said one thing but his stiff body and terse handshake said another. His attitude clicked a thought into place for Kate. Torri bore the same last name as those that had killed his mother and brothers.

"Hmmm." The woman actually purred. "Love the accent. And the pleasure's *all mine.*"

Kate wouldn't have been surprised had Torri gone into a writhing orgasm then and there on the sidewalk. Darach regained his hand and wrapped his arm around Kate again.

"You are gorgeous." She visually ate him up. Kate wasn't given to violence, but she had a terrible itch to slap the lasciviousness off the other woman's face. Torri shot Kate an arch look. "I can see why you've been hiding him from the rest of us." Men seemed blind to Torri's cattiness, but Kate very clearly read Torri's incredulity that Darach was with her. "What a shame. Kate said you're leaving town tomorrow."

"Nae. I will be here a fortnight." Thank you, MacTavish. He wanted Torri to know he'd be around? Kate felt as if he'd dashed cold water in her face. "Mayhap, 'tis her other man who is on his way out of town, eh, Katie?"

"Right." She laughed up at him for Torri's benefit. "You know you're the only one, darling."

Torri totally ignored Kate and sent her mane flying once again. Amazing that she didn't have a chronic neck condition. "Really? For two weeks. That's fabulous. Where are you staying?"

"Why, with Katie, of course."

"I know she keeps a busy schedule. Give me a call. I'd be glad to show you around the city." She looked at Kate. "Anything to help a friend." Uh-huh. And Kate would love to invest in some oceanfront property in Kansas. Torri stroked Darach's left arm. "I know how time can drag when you're alone with nothing fun to do."

"You are a good friend to Katie to offer—"

What? If he...

"—but I need that time when she is at work. Keep it to yourself," he lowered his voice as if sharing a secret—Torri leaned in closer, "because I would rather the other lads not know, but she fair wears me out and I need that time to recover." His intimate smile, now aimed at Kate, was obviously that of a lover. For a second it was just the two of them when she smiled back at him. Darach glanced back at Torri. "I am not complaining, no man would, but my Katie-love is a lusty wench."

Torri's face portrayed a fast-action sequence of expressions. Surprise. Consternation. Fury. A tight smile. "Who would've guessed? Well, if you get bored or lonely, just give me a call. I'm in the book."

"I dunnae think so."

Torri turned on her heel and marched down the sidewalk.

"I dinnae like her. She is a bluidy Campbell and you cannae trust her, Katie. I dinnae like the way she looked at you. That is why I told her I would be here a fortnight."

Darach, ever the protector—except Kate didn't need protecting from anyone, not even Torri. Delighted by his response, Kate laughed. "I certainly didn't like the way she looked at you."

Kate could've kissed him for what he'd just done and said. In fact, that seemed like a grand idea. Despite the fact that they were standing in the middle of the sidewalk in front of her hospital, Kate wrapped her other arm around his neck and kissed him, short and hard and full of promise.

"Your lusty wench is ready to go home," she murmured in his ear.

Darach released her and crossed his arms over his chest.

"Nay, not until I have heard about this other man." Planted in the middle of the sidewalk, he looked about as tractable as dried glue.

Was that a note of jealousy or insecurity or perhaps both? "There is no other man."

"Then who was she talking about? You told her you had a man who was leaving after tonight?"

Why did he have to remember that part? This was going to be more than a little embarrassing and slightly complicated. Not the discussion to have on the sidewalk of Peachtree Street on a busy Friday evening.

"This isn't exactly the place to discuss it. I'll explain on the way home."

They made it to the parking garage without running into anyone else Kate knew. She'd barely closed the car door, and hadn't gotten as far as the key in the ignition, when Darach said, "How could I have been the man you were meeting earlier since you had no inkling you were going back in time to Scotland? You had not even met me."

Torri would've probably run with his assumption there was another man on the scene. And while it would probably be good for the arrogant laird of Glenagan to think he wasn't the only man in her life, it wasn't Kate's style.

"Just listen for a minute, okay?" The dome light went out and she welcomed the dark as she brought him up to speed.

"I knew tonight was the last night before the exhibit closed. I felt foolish that I kept going to see your portrait, even though I was the only one that knew. I was in the doctor's lounge freshening up when Torri came in. You've seen first-hand how catty she can be. She had an audience so she started needling me as to whether I was getting ready for a date, fully expecting that I didn't have one." God, she was about to sound truly foolish and juvenile. "I knew I was going to see you so you became my date. I told her you traveled and would be leaving town after tonight."

Darach stared at her for a moment and then he threw back his head and laughed. "Aye, Kate, you are a clever lass *and* a lusty wench. Let's go home."

10

"HERE WE ARE. This is my condo. Just a second," she said, fitting her key in the lock.

They'd taken that thing she'd called a car, which was a very elegant carriage that moved without benefit of horses, left it in a cave she called a parking garage, climbed flights of stairs and now they were almost in her home, a place inside a maze of a building.

'Twas not a minute too soon. Darach fair ached with the need to have her, especially after she'd confessed to visiting his portrait often, fantasizing about him, and then making him out to be a real man, *her* man, to that harridan they'd met outside. She had but to look at him to know he existed... somewhere. He had only to smell her scent, to feel a brush of her skin against his and he wanted her.

He cupped her buttocks from behind and squeezed. Not a grab as she'd done with him on the street corner, but slower, more of a caress. She slanted a glance over her shoulder.

"I couldnae help myself," Darach said, echoing her earlier explanation for grabbing him.

"You'd use my own words against me." She laughed, an edgy breathy sound, and opened the door. "Here it is. Home sweet home."

He followed her in. At a glance, he took measure of the room. Pale orange, the sky's hue when dawn crept over the moor, washed her walls. Bookcases, full of neatly organized books, lined a wall. A desk boasting clean, simple lines stood in one corner and the wall opposite the door was naught but glass, the city glowing beyond. Worn wood covered her floor. 'Twas vastly different from his castle, yet he knew a sense of home, of recognition. It felt of Katie. It contained her scent.

"I leave a couple of lights on timers so they'll come on before I get home," she said, indicating a lamp that glowed in the corner of the room. "I hate walking into a dark room."

He dropped the satchel containing his kilt and boots on the floor. "I dunnae care about the lights." He wrapped his fingers about her arms and pulled her to him.

"Me either." Her keys and satchel joined his on the floor. She fitted her body against his, linking her arms about his neck. The feel of her in his arms fair drove him to madness. He buried his hands in her curls and kissed her with a need bordering on pain.

He felt as if he'd lost a part of himself when he'd crossed to her time. A part that he'd find in her. He hadn't dared touch her since she'd kissed him on the street, but now....

She slid her hand between them and cupped him through his breeches. She broke the kiss. "I've got a reputation as a lusty wench to live up to," she murmured against his mouth.

He responded to her sexy teasing. "You are not angry about that are you, Katie-love?"

"Angry?" She laughed and pressed a kiss to his jaw. "Hardly. I should offer to pay you for saying it."

"Aye. I ken just the payment I favor...." He slid his hand beneath the hem of her shirt, over her smooth skin to the soft fullness of her breast. Her tip pebbled against his hand.

"Oh." She worked the front of his breeches open and slipped her hand inside, her clever fingers stroking his rod through his undergarment. "I always pay my debts."

Aye, she knew just the way to touch him.... "A lusty wench with honor."

She withdrew her hand from his breeches.

"Come upstairs and I'll show you something you'll like."

He was perfectly happy right here. He rolled her nipple beneath two fingers. "I've found something I like here."

"Come on." She tugged him toward the stairs to the left. "I promise you'll enjoy this."

She flipped a switch and small lights lit up along the wall going up the stairs. 'Twas truly amazing that light appeared as though by magic. "We are going up there?"

"Uh-huh."

He reached out and swept her off her feet, holding her close to his chest. Kate laughed and looked up into his face, but he didn't miss the heat and the flash of excitement in her green eyes. "What are you doing?"

"I am carrying a lusty wench up yon stairs to collect my payment." In a fortnight he'd leave her behind and either save his people or die trying. But in the time between, he'd savor every moment with this woman he'd thought he might never see again.

"Because you're a bold brawny Scotsman from the wild Highlands?"

"Aye. We're a savage lot."

"And you're going to give me a Highland fling?"

"And then some, lassie." He reached the top of

the stairs and she pointed to a doorway to the left. "In there."

He entered, discerning the dark outline of the bed from the stairway lights. He tossed her atop the mattress and she rolled over with a laugh. He loved to hear her laugh and he loved to know he was the one making her laugh.

A click sounded and her bedside lantern cast light over ivory walls and a pale coverlet on her bed. "Take your clothes off, Darach. I need you naked for your surprise."

"You dunnae have to ask twice. I can finally… how did you phrase it…turn my big boy loose."

Her laugh, heated, breathy feathered over him. "There wasn't time to argue the point. You needed to get dressed and we needed to get out of there." She knelt on the bed and undressed. More than once he had to remind himself to quit looking and undress so they could get to what they both wanted.

She got off the bed, took him by the hand and led him into an adjoining room. "This is the bathroom."

Once again, as before, the room was lit. Stone-colored tile covered the floor and was cool beneath his bare feet. A large looking-glass reflected both the light and their image. A basin sat in the midst of a marble slab on one wall. A seat that appeared to be a cross between a chamber pot and a throne stood in one corner. A large tub, he assumed for washing, took up one short wall.

She turned him to look behind them. "And this—" she opened a glass door and tugged on a large button and a smaller one beneath it and water flowed through two devices coming out of the mirrored wall "—this is a hot shower."

She stepped inside. "Come on in. The water's fine."

He did her bidding. Warm water sluiced over him in a truly decadent pleasure. He sighed. "Aye. 'Tis like standing beneath a waterfall on a warm day—only better because even on a warm day, the burn runs cold."

"The previous owners were apparently shower enthusiasts. Most aren't this large." Water darkened her hair from flaxen to brown. Her skin gleamed alabaster with the water's sheen. "For the first part of my payment, I thought I'd bathe you."

Standing beneath the water was pleasure in itself. Add to that her hands on his skin. "You'll get no argument from me."

"I'll start with your hair." She picked up a bottle and eyed the shelf that formed a bench on one end of the enclosure. "And I think this will work nicely." She stood up on the tile seat. *"Voilà."*

Her perch brought her lovely breasts to mouth

level. He grasped her at her waist, her skin soft and wet and warm beneath his hands. "Aye, this is grand," he said. He leaned forward and captured one perfect tip in his mouth.

"Darach…" She leaned forward, into him.

He suckled and the bud tightened against his tongue. He slid his hands up her water-kissed skin, over her middle to cup her globes, one in each hand. He moved his attention to the other one, sucking and licking until it too pebbled with need and Kate's sighs echoed off the tile and glass wall. Ah, this was one of the finer things in life, the dual sensations of warm water coursing over his shoulders and down his back, her breasts in his hands and mouth.

She pulled back. "If you keep that up, my legs are going to be too weak to hold me up."

He grinned. "Sorry, Katie-love, it's just that with temptation staring me in the face…." He flicked his tongue against one of her pink pearls.

"Then let's put temptation out of reach." She turned him around to face the mirrored wall and torrent of water.

"I would much rather be looking at your teats than at myself."

"Hush." She laughed and slapped him on his arse.

For one second he was stunned and then he laughed. "God's tooth you are bold, lass. Nary a man nor woman has slapped me on me arse since my Da when I was but a lad."

She smiled, full of sexy sass, over his shoulder at him in the mirror. "Then it's long overdue."

He pretended to scowl at her reflection. "Aye, you've fire enough when my back is turned."

Had he ever made light with a lass this way? Nay. He'd never been so inclined.

Kate buried her fingers in his wet hair and began to work in fragrant soap that smelled faintly familiar. It was her scent, the scent that clung to her skin and hair, the scent that heated him through. She rubbed and kneaded from the front of his head to the back and along his neck. Darach groaned aloud from the pleasure of her fingers dancing against his scalp. "Ah, you've a magic touch, Katie-love."

"I'm glad you like it."

He more than liked it. The warm water and the rhythm of her hands against his scalp and on his shoulders lulled him. Yet in another part of him, her scent and her touch and her very nearness fueled his want for her and hardened his rod.

She kneaded and plied her hands along his arms. She stepped down from the bench and continued stroking his muscles down the length of his back. She worked her hands over his buttocks and the backs of his legs. The saucy wench reached between his legs and cupped his heavy sac and he shuddered at her touch. She stroked his member with her soap-slicked hands, rousing the interest of his rod.

"Mayhap we can run into another harridan of your acquaintance so I can once again earn your indebtedness. I've a definite liking for your payment."

She stroked him again and his cock surged in her hand. "I think that is a fine plan." She reached around him and smoothed her hands over his belly and up his chest, her bare breasts with their tight points pressing against his back. "You are without a doubt, the most perfect specimen of a man I've ever seen."

He knew women looked at him and the women he'd bedded had been free with their flattery. But there'd always been the knowledge, in the back of his mind, that he was their laird and as such, they had a stake in flattering him. But he was no laird to Katie.

He looked over his shoulder with an uncharacteristic self-consciousness. "Ye have obviously forgotten about my scar and my nose."

She traced the scar's path with one finger. "No. I haven't forgotten it at all. I think it's a mark of courage and honor." She turned him to face her and tilted his head back beneath the stream of warm water, rinsing the soap from his hair. "And what's wrong with your nose?"

"'Tis more of a beak than a nose." At least that had been his brothers' take on it when they were lads.

She cupped his jaw in her hand and peered at him, head cocked to one side. "It's strong, like you. I can't imagine your face with anything different. You'd look silly with anything less. As it stands now, you're gorgeous and extremely sexy."

Her words pleased him, warmed him, in a way that had nothing to do with sex. "Katie-love, you're a bit of a daft lass." He teased her to cover how much her words pleased him, but there wasn't much that got by Katie. Her eyes held a knowing look.

"Then I'm in good company 'cause you're one daft Scotsman."

He popped her on her arse. "'Tis bold and brawny, not daft."

She gasped and pretended outrage. "You're pushing your luck, Scotsman."

He hadn't made light like this since the day he'd traded his family and his childhood to the Campbells for the promise of a few more minutes of fun. Aye, his heart had not been this light since.

With a start he realized he'd thought of that time without a blackness settling over his soul. Did she but know it, Kate was a true healer, of not just body, but mind and soul as well.

He shifted closer and caught her up to him, savoring the slide of her wet skin against his. He pressed a kiss to her mouth, his tongue finding and toying with hers. He cupped her arse in his hands and pulled her tighter and harder against him, his cock unerringly finding the curls between her thighs. She wrapped her arms about his neck and pressed against him. With her bottom in his hands, he slid one finger against her slit. Ah, she was wet. Not the wet of streaming water, but the slicker, hotter wet borne of want. He eased a finger into her and she ground down on it, making small noises of pleasure.

"When I first saw your portrait at the museum it…affected me. I was more aroused by you in a picture than I had ever been by a man in real life. Every time I came home from the museum, a terrible lust came with me. But not just for any man. For you." She spoke the truth. She was wet and hot and slick against his finger. "One of my favorite fantasies about us was in here."

She scattered kisses along his jaw and to his ear. Her tongue teased his ear's edge and heat rushed through him. She edged away from his cock, replacing her mound with her hand. She wrapped her fingers around him and stroked while she swirled her tongue about his nipple.

Was there anything more potent to a man's libido than a woman whispering in his ear how much she'd wanted him before she'd even met him? He was more than willing to participate in whatever it was she'd created in her mind.

"And what would that be Katie-love?" He captured a drop of water on her shoulder with his tongue. "Tell me how to make your fantasy come true."

"In my fantasy, you sit here."

He sank onto the warm, wet tile that formed a seat.

"And I just need to make a bit of an adjustment here." She turned off the upper shower and adjusted the lower so that what had been a gentle shower now shot out in a steady, pulsing stream. Facing the mirrored wall afforded him a bonnie view.

Darach expected Katie to mount him and he'd watch in the mirror as she rode him. Instead, she braced her hands on either side of his hips and leaned forward. She stood with her feet braced apart and leaned forward from the hips, offering him a most arousing view of her backside compliments of the mirror. She teased his nipple with the tip of her tongue. Darach dropped his head back against the tiled wall as the sensation of her flirting tongue against his hard nub shot straight to his groin.

She worked her way down, scattering kisses along his belly. God's tooth, was she going to do what he thought she was?

She swirled her tongue along his knob and teased at the slit with the tip of her tongue. "Aye, yes…."

Katie paused and looked up at him with a wicked smile that further tightened his bollocks. "After the trauma of being confined in underwear for all of an hour, I think your big boy needs some special care and attention." She pressed a kiss to his tip.

Yes! He was very willing to play his part in her fantasy so far. Darach nodded. "Aye. He suffered. He's in desperate need."

"So, I see." She licked from the base to the tip and then rimmed her lips back down to his root. She worked her tongue and mouth around his sac before moving back up to his tip.

Her mouth, warm and slick and tight around his rod, embraced him. When she lowered her mouth over him, she hiked her bottom into the air, offering him a reflected view of her pink paradise and opening herself to the stream of water. She slid her mouth up and down, sucking and lapping. And the water massaged her.

Heat exploded in him and rendered his breath

ragged. It was the most arousing thing he'd ever experienced, her hot mouth wrapped around him while the mirror reflected the water pulsing against her lovely glistening folds.

While he could still think with enough coherence to speak, he said, "Aye, Katie-love, I've a definite interest in hearing about all your fantasies."

11

HALF AN HOUR LATER, her hair still damp from the shower, Kate almost pinched herself. Instead, she glanced across her kitchen. Yes. The laird of Glenagan sat on a bar stool while she whipped up a quick meal after great shower sex.

"I think it's almost ready," she said. The slab of thick cheddar oozed past the edge of the bread and sizzled on the griddle. Perfect.

"It smells good," Darach said

She transferred two grilled-cheese sandwiches onto a plate and poured a cup of tomato soup. She placed both on the counter before him. "It's not gourmet by any means, but it's hot."

She served herself and slid onto the leather bar stool next to him. "Go ahead and eat."

Darach bit into the sandwich. "Hmm. It tastes even better than it smells."

She smiled. "It's pretty good but I think shoe leather might taste good to you about now."

Now that she was back in her world and not worried about being stuck in Merry Olde Scotland, she was much less uptight.

Kate wouldn't have been surprised if an awkwardness had settled between them. Instead they enjoyed a companionable silence while they ate. Even though they would've looked like quite the odd couple to anyone looking in—he with his long dark hair and his kilt, she with her short hair and silk pajamas—there was something about traveling two-hundred and sixty-one years with someone in the blink of an eye that forged a bond.

She knew she could fire up her laptop, log on and within minutes details about the Battle of Culloden would appear on the screen. Internet research hovered two clicks away. But not tonight. It had been an incredible day, or couple of days depending on which time continuum she wanted to adhere to, and tomorrow was soon enough. Any information they'd find tonight would still be there tomorrow and she very selfishly wanted this evening without the specter of the future hanging over it.

Darach pointed past her to the reading nook she'd set up in lieu of a dining room table. "Is that woman in the portrait your mother? You look like her."

She turned to the photograph and a familiar sadness welled inside her. "Yes. That's my mom."

His comment surprised her. "Do you really think I look like her?" With her dark hair and laughing green eyes, she seemed to smile right at Kate. "I always thought she was beautiful."

"You are both beautiful. You have the same nose. You both smile with your eyes in the same manner, and you hold your head at that same angle."

His words brought a sense of comfort and she smiled despite the melancholy that ate at her soul. "You would have liked her. Everyone liked her." Kate stood. "She was a remarkable woman. She died a few years ago."

Compassion softened the harsh lines of his face. "What happened?"

Kate rounded the counter and gathered the dishes. "She had breast cancer. They caught it early and we thought she'd beat it, but it came back." She rinsed the plates and bowls and stacked them in the dishwasher.

"What is this breast cancer?"

Oh, yeah, he wouldn't be up to speed on modern health issues. Cancer, named and identified, wasn't part of his world. "Everyone's body is made up of cells. The cells unite to form skin, tissue, organs, blood. When all the cells are healthy and doing their thing, the body is in good shape. But sometimes, and we don't exactly know why, the cells begin to mutate. The mutated cells begin to destroy the good

cells. Sometimes we can stop the bad cells and sometimes we can't. We've already learned so much and
every day we come a little closer to a cure. A cancer
diagnosis used to be a death sentence and sometimes
it still is, but increasingly it's become more of a
matter of managing a chronic—" *would he know
what chronic meant?* "—ongoing illness. You would
know it as a wasting disease. The body wastes away
and the person suffers great pain before they die."
She wiped down the counter, not wanting to
remember what her mother had been like at the end.

"Aye. I have seen something very similar in old
Hattie in the village. Was your mother in great pain?"

"Enough. Even at the end, though, she was
more concerned about me than about herself. She
worried about leaving me. It's terrible to be a
doctor and not be able to do anything to save the
person you love the most."

"Aye." He didn't have to say more. She knew he
was intimately acquainted with the pain of standing
by helpless and watching a loved one die. "This
cancer. Does it spread from person to person?"

"No, it's not contagious. Certain types of cancer
have hereditary factors. My grandmother died of
breast cancer, then my mother. I'm checked each
year because I have a higher risk because of both of
them."

A dark frown knit his brows together. "So, you could have this terrible cancer? And your children?"

She knew he was thinking of that broken condom and the very real possibility she could be pregnant. "I could. And yes, it would be a factor if I ever had a daughter, but it's not something to dwell on." She shrugged. "I could also be hit by a car the next time I'm crossing the street. I have regular check-ups. I take care of myself. Other than that, there's nothing more to do than go on with my life."

"Do you have brothers and sisters? What about your father?"

"I'm an only child. I was just a baby when my father died. He was a doctor, too. He was part of a relief team flying into Turkey after an earthquake. His plane crashed into a mountain." She'd always wished for even a vague memory of the serious man she only knew from photographs. "All my life it was just me and my mother."

He reached out and plied his thumb against the back of her hand, his touch carrying a comfort, a re-assurance. "And now it is just you?"

Wasn't that what she'd thought earlier in the evening, before she'd fallen back through time? "I suppose. But I have my job." And she always pulled the rotations at Christmas and Thanksgiving. "It's not just a job, it's who I am. Sort of like you. You're the laird, but it's not just a title and it's not just a job you show up for at eight in the morning and leave behind when you get through at five. It defines who you are, what you are, how you live, and the choices you make."

It didn't matter that they came from different backgrounds, different countries, different professions, different centuries. Kate knew there'd never been a man who understood her more than this one. Despite their differences, they came from the same place.

"Truer words were ne'er spoken. And why is there no husband, no bairns in your life?"

"My job is busy, demanding, and the hours are crazy." And those were all excuses, soundbites. There had been the oblique pain of never knowing a father and the acute pain of losing a mother who was everything. Why not find the courage to give it voice? "And because I've already lost enough. I don't want to lose again."

"Aye." Darach stood and drew her into the temporary comfort of his arms. He cradled her head to his chest and she rested her cheek against his warm skin, soaking up his solace. Beneath her cheek, his heart beat sure and steady.

She accepted the comfort he offered. She'd be alone again soon enough.

DARACH AWOKE, ALONE, in Katie's bed. Last night she'd thrown his plaid atop her bed to remind him of home. He hadn't had the heart to tell her that wasn't proper and he'd left it be. Now Glenagan's scent mingled with the scent of Katie and her home into a most soothing blend.

He stretched, enjoying her soft sheets against his bare skin. It had been a pleasure previously unknown to drift off to sleep with his lass in his arms. He'd never spent the night in a woman's bed or had one spend the night in his. It had started out as a cautionary measure and turned into a habit—one he'd not had a hard time developing as he'd never particularly felt a desire to spend the night with a woman. But he held no enemies in this place and time and it had been a sweet pleasure to feel the beat of Katie's heart against the arm that he'd curled around her, the warmth of her breath against his neck, the press of her soft curves against him and her scent wrapped around him.

Something nagged at the back of his mind. Something was different other than the obvious circumstances of being in a different place and time. What was missing? He tried to put his finger on what it was, but it eluded him. With a shrug he rolled out of bed and visited her bathroom. This was a hell of an improvement over a chamber pot and a cold basin. He belted his kilt in place and went in search of Katie, following his nose to an aroma that fired his appetite.

He walked down the hall, the wood floor cool beneath his feet, but not nearly as cold as Glenagan's stones. He found her ensconced in a wide green chair in the great room that also housed her kitchen. She had what appeared to be a large book turned sideways opened on her lap.

She looked up as he padded into the kitchen. "Hi. Did you rest okay? You were sound asleep when I got up."

Ah. It clicked into place—the thing that was missing. The nightmare that visited him every evening had not come calling last night. For the first time in six and twenty years, his family's death hadn't haunted his sleep. "I slept like a bairn. 'Tis a fact you've a bed more to comfort than mine."

"I'm glad it was comfortable for you." She placed the thing that wasn't a book after all on the footstool and stood.

"I've made some coffee. Eggs sound okay for breakfast?"

"I'm partial to whatever you prepare." He didn't want to burden her while he was here.

Darach leaned against the counter and watched as she moved about the room. She moved with an economy and purpose he admired. But last night's playfulness had vanished. It wasn't as much a stiffness of manner he discerned as a distance.

She brought a cup of fragrant black brew and placed it on the counter beside him. "Your coffee, MacTavish. Be careful you don't burn yourself. It's hot."

She started to move away and he wrapped one arm about her waist, pulling her back against him. "What's the matter this morning, Katie-love? Do you already regret bringing me back with you?"

She glanced up at him, her eyes guileless. "No, not at all. I think last night I was punch drunk—giddy I'd made it back and managed to bring you with me. Last night I managed to avoid thinking about today or tomorrow or the spring." She looked away from him, her tone somber. "But this morning I read about the Battle of Culloden. It was very sobering." She rested her head against his breast, muffling her words but not the underlying quiet anguish. "It was terrible and twice as much so to imagine you there."

His heart jolted in his chest at her admission of caring. He tilted her face up and pressed a kiss to the edge of her hair. "Not to worry. If I'm to have a fortnight here, then I dunnae want your heart heavy on my behalf. The battle isn't fought yet and the deed is not done." He interjected a teasing note.

"Now are you trying to starve me to death before the Sassenach can have a go at me? Where is my morning meal, wench?" He slapped her on the arse, just for good measure.

She laughed, as he'd intended, but the look in her eye said she knew exactly what he was about. Katie-love was one clever lass. "Keep that up you Scots barbarian and you'll find yourself wearing breakfast instead of eating it."

While she went about the business of preparing the food and throughout the meal, she explained yet two more marvels of modern technology—something called the computer and the Internet.

'Twas amazing the number of things that made modern life so much easier than in his time. At Glenagan, he was waited on as befitted his title and that was the job of the people that worked in his house. But this wasn't Glenagan and it wasn't Katie's job so the laird of Glenagan helped clean up the kitchen—which was easy with what she called a dishwasher.

Kate took him by the hand and led him to the seating area. "Come on. I'll show you the laptop," Katie said. "Go ahead and take the chair."

He sank into the chair she'd had earlier. Katie perched on the arm and he tried to focus on her instructions but having her hip against his arm, her shoulder next to his, proved distracting. She opened what he'd thought to be a book when he'd first walked into the room and placed it in his lap—even more distracting. Ah, so this was a laptop. Made perfect sense to him since she'd placed it on his lap.

She paused in her instructions. "I just thought about it…do you know how to read? If you don't it's not a problem."

Darach chuckled. On one hand she knew things about him none other knew—she knew of his nightmare and his shame. She knew how he looked when he slept. Yet there was much she didn't know as well.

"Aye. Even the Scots barbarian has a bit of schooling. I read Gaelic, English and Latin. I even know how to do a bit of sums. Da insisted. He believed if I could read, write and do sums, 'twould be much harder for my enemies to take advantage of me and Glenagan. 'Twas good advice."

Kate nodded. "My mother always said knowledge couldn't be taken away from me."

She showed him how to search the Internet and then how to access files resulting from that search. Within minutes he was comfortable with it.

"You're a quick study," she said.

He winked at her. "Aye. But do not tell anyone.

I do not want to ruin my reputation as a brawny bar-barian."

Katie laughed and stood. 'Twas but one of the things he liked about her—she laughed at him, with him.

"I think there are several hours of reading for you there. Would you mind if I went out for a while? I have some errands and…well, I thought you might want some privacy."

"I'll be fine. Don't worry about me."

"Drinks are in the fridge. Help yourself to whatever you want." She wrote on a note pad on the table next to the chair and handed him the sheet of paper. She also handed him an object he'd never seen before. "Here's the phone if you need me. Push this button, hold it up to your ear like this and when you hear the buzzing sound punch in these numbers. That's my cell phone number and I'll have it on." She put the phone back in its holder. "If you promise not to leave my condo, I won't tie you to my bed— which is, I've found, your standard procedure for keeping someone in a room."

"Nay, there's no need to tie me to your bed." He raised his eyebrows suggestively, "I will wager that can keep until you get back."

She paused as if she was about to say something

but instead merely bent down and kissed him hard. "I'll be back."

"I'll be here."

He waited until the door clicked shut behind her before he got down to the business of reading about the battle in which he died and his clan had ultimately perished.

12

KATE PAUSED in the stairwell leading to the parking garage. She fished the number out of her purse and punched it into her cell. Hamish answered on the third ring.

"Hamish? Kate Wexford."

"And what can I do for you this fine morning, Dr. Wexford? Did you and Darach have some questions for me? I'm not sure I'll have answers, but I'll try."

"Uh, this is a little more personal in nature."

He chuckled on the other end. "Okay. I'll be interested in what's more personal than time travel."

"Shopping." She felt a bit ridiculous. "I…um…I didn't know how busy you were, but I wandered if you…um, might be available for some power shopping. I think you have a good eye—the suit you picked out for Darach was perfect for him."

"Thank you. I'd like to think I've a bit of an eye for fashion. And I'm wide open until one this afternoon. Who are we shopping for?"

"I was hoping to pick up a few things for both Darach and myself."

"Darach is going *shopping?*"

Kate laughed. "No, Darach is Internet surfing. But he's going to be here for two weeks. He'll go stir-crazy in my condo and I think he's going to need more than his kilt and one suit. I want to show him everything. I was thinking some casual wear for him, but he doesn't strike me as the type of man who'd enjoy a shopping trip so I thought I'd surprise him."

"I'm your man. Where do you want to meet and when?"

"I thought Atlantic Station. Want me to swing by and pick you up?"

"No. I'll cab it there. It's easier that way. I can be there in half an hour."

They agreed on a meeting point and Kate continued down the stairs to the parking garage. She'd come to an important decision. Darach was here for two weeks, then he'd go back to Scotland and the eighteenth century forever, possibly to an imminent death.

She turned left out of the building and navigated the familiar streets. The way she saw it, she had two choices. She could sit around, morose for the next two weeks. Or she could make the next two weeks a memorable adventure for both of them—two weeks they'd never forget, even with hundreds of years separating them.

She parked and killed a few minutes window shopping. She snuggled deeper into her jacket. The wind held a definite chill today.

"Hi, Kate," Hamish said from behind her.

She turned and returned his greeting. For all that Hamish seemed to have an eye for fashion, he certainly didn't turn it on himself. Much as at the museum, he wore a long sleeved shirt and a pocketed vest with nondescript trousers and brown lace-up shoes. He looked like a frumpy sixty-something year old man.

"Thanks for meeting me on such short notice. I thought Darach could use some time alone to digest the information and I thought some comfortable casual clothes would be a nice surprise."

"A very nice surprise." His blue eyes danced with excitement. Go figure, a man with a passion for shopping.

Hamish proved to be a power shopper. An hour later, Kate once again swiped her debit card.

"You've spent a bit of money today," Hamish said.

Kate looked at the shopping bags they'd amassed in a short period of time and shrugged. "I inherited money from both my parents. And I make more than enough at my job. It's something I want to do for him." How could she begin to explain the connection she felt to Darach in such a short period of time when she didn't quite understand it herself? "I want to make this a special time for him."

Hamish looked at her and offered a crooked smile but said nothing as they walked out of the store. A coffee shop beckoned from next door.

"How about a coffee before we call it a day?" Kate suggested.

"Sure, I could go for a biscotti too," Hamish said, already opening the door.

They entered and Kate inhaled the fragrant blends. She seriously thought she might be addicted to the stuff. Forget the biscotti, she wanted a cup of java. They ordered and settled at a small corner table.

She took a couple of fortifying sips and finally found the nerve to ask the question that had nagged at her throughout the morning. "Hamish?"

"Yes?" He glanced up from dunking the biscotti in his coffee.

"Did you die at Drumossie that day?"

"Nay." His soft answer was almost lost in the quiet jazz piped in as background music and the other conversations around them. He took a bite and chewed thoughtfully for a minute or two. Kate let the silence stretch between them. "I was wounded and had taken refuge at a farmer's croft. The British hunted me down, me and others like me. They lined us up against a wall and shot us."

Kate had read the accounts but to hear it first-hand…her stomach plummeted. "I'm sorry. And I'm sorry I asked. I'm sure it's not something you care to remember."

He munched another bite of the coffee-soaked cookie. "It's okay. I've died many times before in many places. It's not my death that's difficult. Dying is much easier than watching those you love die and being powerless to help them."

Part of her wanted to know about Darach, wanted to ask about his death. Another part of her couldn't bring herself to because hearing it via a first-hand account made it real. Besides, Hamish had just said it was difficult to watch friends die, how could she possibly ask him about….

"You want to know about Darach?"

She smoothed a crumb off the table. "Yes. No. I don't know. Okay. If it's not too painful for you to talk about, I suppose I'd rather know than not know."

"We went into battle together. Darach knew it was a useless endeavor. We'd marched all night. We were weary and outnumbered. He tried to persuade our regiment leader to allow the men to rest. But

Charles had already made up his mind that we'd fight that day. So we scrugged our bonnets, checked our pistols and fought like madmen. It took six dragoons to bring him down. Many more than that fell before his sword." Even now, nearly three centuries later, his voice rang with pride in the fight Darach MacTavish had fought.

"Did he just go down injured? Maybe if there was medical attention…."

"No." Hamish caught her hand in his, something akin to pity shadowing his eyes. "There was nothing to be done, Kate. They cut his head off."

Kate was glad he held her hand in his, otherwise she wasn't sure she could've contained the anguish that welled inside her. Her head swam, feeling very light, dizzy. She leaned forward and shoved her head between her knees, dragging in deep breaths. When she no longer felt as if she might pass out at the table, she slowly sat up.

Hamish waited calmly until she raised her head.

"I'm sorry," she said.

"You've nothing to be sorry for. It's difficult to hear news of someone you love dying violently. But you need to remember, he may not be able to change a major historical event, but he can change his own outcome. He need not die at Drumossie."

Kate had been attracted to Darach, well, to his

portrait, for months. But once she'd met him she'd discovered he was more than just a wickedly sexy Highlander. He was a man of integrity, strength, power coupled with tenderness and compassion.

Now she wasn't sure which surprised her the most, to discover she was in love with a man she'd only just met and who belonged in the eighteenth century, or that he didn't necessarily have to die.

DARACH PUT ASIDE Kate's laptop and stood, stretching his muscles. 'Twas a grim account indeed. As Katie had relayed, it hadn't simply been an end to his life, it had marked the end to Scotland's clans.

He'd found answers to many of the questions he'd posed to Katie, yet he was no closer to knowing how to change the course of history.

Years of being chieftain had taught him a valuable lesson. Often the harder you looked at a problem, the more the answer hid.

When would Katie be home? He was glad she'd left. What he'd read…the end of not just his life but a way of life as he knew it…he was glad she'd left him to his own company. But now he missed her. Missed her laughter, her smile, the sound of her voice, the sparkle and intelligence in her green eyes.

He walked to the window, where sunlight poured in and pooled on the wooden floor. He looked out on the city that was her world. Buildings loomed near and in the far distance. Katie lived in a land of castles. 'Twas an odd thought that Hamish now lived, quite happily it would seem, in this land as well.

By rights he should feel at odds here, but strangely he didn't. Mayhap because this was Katie's home and he was surrounded by her things and her scent. Was it possible he'd only met her a few days ago?

As if his thoughts had conjured her, her key scraped in the lock. He crossed the room as she came through the door. She carried several parcels in both hands. As if she'd done it countless times before, she toed the door closed behind her.

"Hello." Her smile greeted him and suddenly his heart felt lighter, the day brighter.

"What have you got there? Did you leave wares for anyone else?"

"Believe it or not, I managed to leave a couple of things for other people. Do you know who all of this is for?" She fair danced from one foot to the other, reminding him of a small child at Michaelmas. "You."

"Me?" Darach didn't try to mask his surprise. "Why would you buy me gifts?"

"Because you'll go stir-crazy if you have to stay

in my condo for two weeks." She placed the packages on the floor, tugging on his plaid as she straightened up. "As handsome as you are in your kilt, you'll draw too much attention that way and as great as that suit that Hamish bought looks on you, I thought you might want something more comfortable. I called Hamish, he met me, and we picked up a couple of things for you."

Something warm and wonderful bloomed inside him that she'd take her time to do that for him. He caught her up to him. "You're a daft lass, Katie-love."

"Humph. So far I'm daft, lusty, and clever. You're painting quite a picture, MacTavish."

He framed her face with his hands. "Aye, 'tis a lovely picture. 'Twas my lucky day when you wanted me so much you jumped into a portrait to get into my bed."

"Get it straight, you egomaniac. I didn't jump. I was pushed. Shoved, no less."

Aye, he liked teasing her. "It matters not whether you were a tad clumsy or Hamish a tad overzealous, 'twas all to my good fortune." He kissed the spot just below her ear and she quivered beneath his lips.

"You know, for a barbarian, you have quite a sweet way with words." She linked her arms about his waist, caressing the naked flesh of his back. An aching need blossomed inside him. Would he ever get his fill of this woman? Would he ever know a time when her touch, her scent didn't awaken his hunger for her?

"And for a lusty, clever, daft wench, I am thinking you are wearing too many clothes." He tugged her shirt out of her waistband while he sampled the sweetness of her neck.

"Exactly what did you have in mind, Highlander?"

Without forethought, he knew exactly what he wanted.

"I want to make love to you there, where the sun slants in through the window. I want to lay with you in the warmth of the sun." He skimmed his hand over her flaxen curls. "I want to see the sunlight in your hair—" he shadowed her cheek with his fingertips and down to the length of her neck "—and across your bare skin." Want and need imbued his voice with a hoarseness. "I want to see your face when you find your pleasure with me."

Katie brushed her lips across his chest and a thrill coursed through him. "I think that can be arranged."

KATE STRETCHED LIKE A lazy cat where she lay on the floor in the sun's warmth. She propped on one arm and looked down at Darach on his back, one arm thrown over his face, his breath still uneven.

The sun glinted off his hair, as blue-black as a raven's wing. A smattering of dark hair and corded muscles covered his chest, belly and thighs. His erection, spent but still at half-mast, lay thick and heavy against his thigh.

Dear God, she loved him. Not simply for the breadth of his shoulders or the handsome cragginess of his face or even the sex that was like nothing she'd experienced before. She also loved him for his arrogance, the tenderness he hid beneath his fierce exterior, his unswerving devotion to his people, his playfulness. He was as much an overachiever as she was, and while she might not appreciate the resulting actions, such as tying her to his bed, she understood his motivation.

As if aware of her silent study, he lowered his arm and looked at her. His dark hooded eyes gleamed with satisfaction. Fine lines bracketed the corner of his eyes.

Kate reached out and traced a lazy pattern through the swirls of black hair, down the muscled plane of his belly with one finger, compelled to touch him, to mark the moment as real and because she felt slightly empty with him no longer inside her.

"I have to work tomorrow," she said, lamenting aloud.

She loved her job. She ate, slept, breathed her job.

But for the first time ever she wasn't looking forward to going in and dealing with the non-stop pace of one of Atlanta's busiest ERs. She very selfishly wanted to spend every minute of the next two weeks with Darach before they made the trip from Atlanta to the exhibit's new opening in New York City. She'd look at the schedule and see if she could manage to take off an extra day. Of course, Torri would know exactly why and gleefully tell all. And what difference would that make? Kate was in good standing. She needn't worry if she manipulated an extra day or two off.

"'Tis to be expected." Still flat on his back, he pulled her over to rest against his chest, his arm about her shoulders. Once upon a time she might've been self-conscious about laying on the floor naked, warmed by a shaft of sunlight, the scent of their recent lovemaking clinging to them like a bewitching perfume. Now, it felt like the most natural thing in the world. "Tell me about your job," he said.

She didn't get the impression he asked out of politeness. She didn't think polite registered high on his list. If he asked, he really wanted to know.

Crossing her arms on his broad chest, she rested her chin on top of her hands. He was good sprawling material. "It's hectic and fast-paced. I work 12-hour shifts, rotating days and nights. We have to be prepared for anything and we get a little bit of everything—gunshot wounds, stabbings, abdominal pain, broken bones, burns, domestic abuse—"

"What is that?"

"When someone in a household, usually a husband or a boyfriend, beats up on someone else, usually a woman." She watched him, gauging his reaction. He was, after all, a man who lived in a time when women were chattel and a man's power absolute. Even with her limited background in history she knew that.

A dark frown furrowed his brow. "Aye. There are men who would strike a woman. I have no tolerance for that and I do not allow it in my clan. 'Tis bad practice. 'Tis a man's duty to protect what is his."

Kudos to him on the first point, that he didn't tolerate wife beating among his people. His second point left her wincing. He was obsessive about his role of protector.

"Luckily we don't see very many domestic-abuse cases."

He brushed his big hand over her hip and her skin tingled at the contact. "Could I come with you one day and observe what you do?" he asked.

Kate found his interest in her job immensely flattering. "No. I'm afraid the only way you could actually see me at work was to come in with an emergency problem and we'd rather not go there. But there's a television program that comes fairly close to what it's like. I'll pick up a season of it and we can watch the DVD."

"I would like that." His hand traveled up her back as if he too was driven to touch her. "I'd like to see what you do."

"We can pick it up today. I thought we'd visit the library and the bookstore this afternoon. We can pick up books on Scottish history and…the battle."

"That is a perfect plan."

"You read on-line?"

"I did." He closed his eyes briefly, as if to shut out what he'd read, his pain nearly palpable. "'Twas a dark day for my people."

"I know." She couldn't imagine what it must have been like for him to read about the destruction of so many he knew and loved and had sworn to protect. To see his way of life reduced to a few sad sentences in a history book. She curved the back of her hand against his cheek, offering her understanding and support. "Did you find anything useful in coming up with an alternative?"

His jaw tightened and beneath her his heart beat more rapidly. "The hardest part is I don't exactly know what I am looking for. It could be anything or…it could be nothing. Mayhap there is no clue."

For a moment his eyes, mired in ineffable sorrow, looked old beyond his years. "Mayhap there is no changing the fate of the clan MacTavish."

She protested instinctively. "I can't believe that. I won't believe that. I refuse to believe I took that journey only to hand you a death sentence."

"Mayhap not." Resolution replaced sorrow. "That is why I will continue to search."

She knew him well enough to know he'd move heaven and earth to find a way to save his people, his instinct to protect was so strong. But it wasn't a role he'd been born to, not as the third son. All her life she'd wanted to be a doctor. What had he dreamed of when he was young, before life had thrust him into the dual roles of avenger and protector? "Darach, when you were young, you had two older brothers who were both in line ahead of you to be laird. Before…that day, what did you want to do? What did you want to be when you grew up?"

"'Twas a long time ago…" He stared at the ceiling but she doubted if he even saw the pipes running along the beams.

"Yes?" she prompted.

"When I was a lad I wanted to be a poet."

Although she smiled, inside Kate's heart wept for the boy who wanted to write poetry but instead took up arms.

13

DARACH SET ASIDE the leather-bound journal Katie had surprised him with the day after he'd confessed his boyhood dream of being a poet.

The last four days had taken on a most pleasant rhythm. He missed Katie when she was away, as if a part of him had gone missing.

Yet it was as if he'd discovered new parts of himself in the meantime. He'd discovered a deep and abiding love of history and poetry. He filled his days reading numerous volumes of history, most enjoying the accounts of the Scottish Enlightenment, a period that had immediately followed his death. He read everything he could find by Hume and Smith and the poets Macpherson, the ill-fated Chatterton, Robert Burns, and Sir Walter Scott.

'Twas as if drenching rains had begun to fill an empty well inside him. In the solitude of the days and nights when Katie was gone he began to fill empty pages with his own poems that seemed to pour forth from him.

He levered himself out of the green chair. He wanted to surprise her. He checked the stainless steel clock mounted on the kitchen wall.

Aye. He'd lost himself in his journal and fanciful thoughts. He'd hurry or he'd be out of time. He loaded a Diana Krall CD in the player—absolutely mind-boggling technology—and got busy in the kitchen.

In a very short period of time he'd developed a weakness for CNN news, jazz vocals, the Fulton County Public library, and double lattes. Likewise, he'd discovered he couldn't abide traffic, soap operas, or fast food.

Hamish had spent a couple of afternoons with him while Katie was at work. The first day Hamish had Darach's picture taken. Yesterday he'd presented Darach with a passport for their upcoming air travel to New York—he'd actually fly like Icarus. Katie had suggested they not question Hamish's connections or methods.

Darach shook his head as he thought of Hamish's idiosyncrisies. Hamish definitely had a weakness for shopping which he, Darach couldn't quite grasp. God's tooth, the man spent an inordinate amount of time and money ordering *stuff* from the shopping network which Darach found vastly amusing considering that Hamish, of all people, should realize he couldn't take it with him.

Darach pulled out the pans and organized them according to the recipe instructions he'd printed off the Internet. He mixed and measured and thought of Kate.

He had a passion for history and poetry and he'd enjoyed getting to know Hamish in a different time and place, but his favorite time was that he spent with Katie. It mattered not whether they were out and about in the city taking in a movie or another marvel, or whether they were lying about in her home talking.

They talked for hours on end about everything, her about growing up without her father, him about growing up without his mother, books, music. She loved science, he loved history, but still they found an interest in the other's opinion.

And the lovemaking, the intimacy of being with her, was beyond what he'd ever imagined it would be. Holding her when she went to sleep at night. Waking up with her leg thrown across his, her hair standing on her head at odd angles, the sleepy way she smiled her pleasure at him with the dawn of each day. With each day, each hour, each passing glance, each caress, she became more precious to him.

And like a spell cast by an enchantress, the days

had flown by with no answer for his past making itself known to him. Instead each day seemed to issue louder the siren's call to leave the past where it lay and make this his future.

And what if Katie was pregnant? What if even now, their bairn grew inside her? If that were the case, would he have the strength to leave her, leave their child and return to his past? Even without a child, how was he to bear leaving this woman who'd come to be as essential to him as the very air he breathed?

He put the thought from his mind and got on with preparing her special meal. The timer had just gone off when she walked through the door.

"Honey, I'm home. What the—?"

Darach glanced around. "I cooked dinner for you. The kitchen is a bit of a mess." He looked at the pots and pans littering the stove and counter and sink. How exactly had things gotten to be such a mess? He'd used every pan in her kitchen. He winced. "Aye. 'Tis more than a mess. I've created a disaster."

"You cooked dinner for me?"

Mayhap she wasn't too upset about his messy kitchen? "Aye. You said last night that meatloaf, mashed potatoes, green beans and peach cobbler always reminded you of your mother and made you feel safe."

She looked from him to the disaster of a kitchen and back. "The laird of Glenagan, chieftain of the clan MacTavish cooked my favorite dinner for me because it makes me feel safe?" Tears swam in the green pools of her eyes and his heart clenched.

He gathered her to him and held her close. "Nay, love. Don't cry. 'Twas meant to make you feel good."

She laughed and dashed away the tears. "I'm crying because I do feel good you crazy Scot."

Time was fleeting and they had but few days together. It seemed the most natural thing in the world to tell her what was in his heart, the heart he'd thought long dead until her. He knew she had regard for him, but it mattered not if she felt the same, he still felt compelled to tell her how he felt. "Did you but know it, I would crawl to Hades and back for you. I never knew I could love anyone the way I love you Katie Wexford." He'd not thought his heart could feel any fuller, but saying the words aloud made him feel… "I love you, you daft, crazy, lusty wench."

She looked up at him, her eyes sparkling with the residual of unshed tears and dawning joy. She cupped her hands about his jaw. "I traveled over two-hundred years to find you. You're everything I never wanted in a man—arrogant, bossy, too sexy for your own good, and gone in less than a week.

How could I not love you with every fiber of my being?"

Her lips brushed his. The kiss deepened and it became a pledge of love that transcended time.

"Make love to me, Darach MacTavish."

His body quickened in ready response. "I'm more than willing, but dinner…"

She laughed softly against his mouth. "Didn't you know meatloaf is best reheated?"

A WEEK AND TWO DAYS after Darach's arrival into the twenty-first century, Hamish sat at dinner with his friend and the man he'd called laird in another time and place, Kate, and Harriett, a recently divorced docent he'd met while at the museum. Darach had assimilated into modern Atlanta amazingly well. Perhaps not that amazing really, Hamish reflected, since life was much easier now, even with global warming and hip-hop.

"Here's to old friends and new beginnings," Hamish said, offering a toast across the white-clothed table. Darach, Kate, and Harriet all raised their champagne glasses and joined in the toast over the flickering candlelight.

Hamish looked pointedly at Darach—that was his cue.

"Tell me again how ya'll know one another,"

Harriett said, precluding Darach and unwittingly throwing a spanner in the works.

"We go way back," Hamish said. Aye, Harriet had no idea. Kate's eyes met his across the table, laughing at his inside joke.

"We share a common interest in history," Darach deadpanned, tugging at his tie. Aye, the man was nervous. As well he should be. Hamish had encouraged him to choose a private moment but Darach wouldn't hear of it, saying Hamish was the reason he and Kate had met in the first place. Harriett, very attractive at fifty-five, evened out the numbers.

While there was a certain *je ne sais quoi* to living in various time periods on different levels, it got lonely. Hamish dated casually, but there was no point in ever letting things get too far between him and a woman. He was destined to live alone and that but doubled his pleasure in Kate and Darach's happiness.

Hamish nudged Darach's leg with his foot beneath the table.

Darach cleared his throat and turned red. Hamish couldn't bite back a smirk. Aye, the man could hold off half a dozen dragoons with a broadsword and a claymore, yet one woman had him tied up in knots.

"Uh, Katie-love, am I understanding correctly that you have the next four days off work?" Darach asked.

Kate smiled at him over the edge of her champagne flute. "Yes. Much to Torri's annoyance—she has to cover for me."

"Aye." He threw his napkin on the table and it barely missed knocking over his water glass. He slipped out of his chair and dropped to one knee, nearly upending the chair in the process. For a large man, he'd always moved with grace and precision. Now he was more like the proverbial bull in the china shop. He grasped Kate's hand in his.

"Katie, uh, I mean Kate. Oh, bluidy hell, forget it. Katie-love, 'tis only a bit more than a week since I first met you, yet has been a lifetime that I've waited for you and will be for all eternity that I know you. Will you do me the honor of marrying me? Will you take the name MacTavish for your own?"

Kate glowed. "Darach MacTavish you're arrogant and bossy and I had no idea what my life was missing until I met you." She raised their clasped hands to her lips and pressed a kiss to Darach's knuckles. Beneath the table, Harriet slipped her hand into Hamish's. "I would be honored to marry you and take your name along with my own."

His black brows met over his dark eyes. "Your own?"

"Yes. Wexford-MacTavish," she said.

Darach let go her hand and took his seat. He crossed his arms over his chest.

It was a look Hamish knew well from serving with the laird of Glenagan. Well, this was about to get interesting. Darach, Mr. Eighteenth Century Highlander, had just come face to face with feminist twenty-first-century sensibilities. Harriet squeezed his hand beneath the table and Hamish shifted in his chair. She need not be getting any ideas.

"Is MacTavish not good enough for you?" Darach said, his voice deceptively soft.

Kate lifted her chin, the same look in her eyes as when she'd indulged in the chest-poking at Glenagan. "I'll bear the name MacTavish with pride, but Wexford is the last link I have to my parents. You're a part of me, but so are they."

Darach's expression softened and he uncrossed his arms. "'Tis a point you have. You are a clever wench."

Hamish nodded to himself. That she was. She knew how to handle Darach.

She smiled at him. "That's why you want to marry me."

Darach returned her smile. "Aye." He stared at the lass, as if they were the only two in the room and there was no more business to be done. Hamish nudged his foot beneath the table and Darach looked back at him without comprehension. Poor devil, he was daft about the lass. "The ring, man. Don't forget the ring."

"Aye." Darach fumbled in his pocket and pulled out the jeweler's box they'd commissioned just yesterday and picked up this afternoon. "I got this for you."

The lad was making a hash of this. Darach MacTavish was a babbling mess.

Kate opened the box and stared on an indrawn breath. "It's beautiful. The most beautiful thing I've ever seen."

With a joy on his face so pure, it nearly brought a tear to Hamish's eye, Darach slipped the ring on Kate's finger. Kate was indeed a healer, for Hamish had never thought to see Darach so happy.

Around them, the other diners and the wait-staff burst into applause. Darach nodded, looking as regal as the Highland chieftain he was. "I am the luckiest man I know."

The lad was slated to die in a few months. Hamish didn't think that quite so lucky, but all the better that Darach consider his good fortune in the here and now.

Kate held out her hand and twisted it to admire the ring. Darach had done well.

"It's simply beautiful."

Darach grinned, looking younger and happier than Hamish had thought possible. "The band is platinum—two bands twisted together to form one—like us. The three stones represent the past, the present, and the future. They're blue diamonds which are rare, much like what we have found together. They are the blue of heather on the Scottish moor, the blue of your Georgia sky, and the blue of the MacTavish tartan. The past, the present, the future."

Kate leaned over and pressed a brief, sweet kiss to Darach's mouth. "Thank you, my poet-warrior. It was beautiful before. Now it's even lovelier. But it had to be wildly expensive…how did you—?"

"'Tis taken care of, love," Darach said, sending Hamish a look of gratitude.

Kate wasn't the only one with more money than she knew what to do with. More than one couple had accused him of playing God, which he didn't—that wasn't his domain, but he possessed excellent financial instincts and he played the stock market on a regular basis—and made a killing. Hey, it funded his shopping network spending—he looked across at Darach—and a long-term loan to an old friend. He would've fronted twice that amount to produce the look on Kate and Darach's face. They'd know happiness for such a short period of time he'd gladly do it again.

"So, I was thinking if you did not have any pressing plans, we could get married day after tomorrow," Darach said.

Kate laughed. "One day to plan a wedding? Sure."

"Do you need more time?"

She shook her head, a glimmer of sadness in her eyes. "We all need more time, but I'll make the most of the time I've been given."

Harriet dabbled at her eyes with the corner of her napkin. "Oh, this is the most romantic thing. And I fear I need to repair my make-up. Hamish, would you escort me to the ladies' room?"

She had that look in her eye…that look that women could get that made a man's blood run cold—she had commitment fever. "I fear my gout's acting up—"

"I didn't know you had gout," Harriet said.

"Aye. It can come upon me suddenly." He looked across the table at Darach. Be it the eighteenth century or the twenty-first, a lad should know when a mate needed bailing out.

Darach came to his rescue. He rose from his seat. "I know I am but a poor substitute but I would be honored if you would allow me to accompany you."

"Thank you, kind sir." Harriet took Darach's arm.

Hamish made a mental note to never bring a date

on any future engagement stints. He looked across at Kate. "Congratulations, lass. You've made him happier than I ever thought possible."

"I love him Hamish—like I never thought to love anyone, like I never wanted to love someone, so completely, so infinitely."

"Yes. It's a rare commodity you've found."

"I always thought that people grew to love one another. They formed a relationship and nurtured it. Much like a garden, you sow the seeds, tend it and reap the benefits."

"That's what it's very much like for most people."

"But it wasn't that way. I sowed nothing. I saw him, even before I met him and it was as if I'd tuned into something bigger than myself."

"You found your soulmate, Kate. You had to travel a few hundred years to do it, but you found him. That's a circumstance as rare as your blue diamond. I don't believe you went back to Darach because he needed you to tell him he was to die at Culloden. I believe you went to him because his soul's need to heal was so powerful it sought you."

She twisted the ring on her finger and looked past him to where Darach waited outside the ladies' lounge. "What happens if he doesn't go back Hamish? What if he stayed? What if he just checked out of the eighteenth century?"

"You know that's not possible, Kate." His heart ached for her. For both of them.

"Why not? He's so smart, he could get a history degree and teach. He could explore his poetry. We could have such a good life. Why isn't it possible?"

"It's not physically impossible but emotionally and mentally it would destroy him. He could stay here and yes, he could possibly teach, own a business—Darach could do pretty much whatever he made up his mind to do. But his people would die. They would perish in the same manner as the accounts you read. And that's what he couldn't live with, Kate. And I don't think you could either. Would you have him stay at the cost of destroying the man you love?"

"You know the answer to that."

He hated the bleakness in her eyes. "Yes. Just as you've known he can't stay and why. Were he to stay, he'd forfeit his honor and no longer be the man you love."

"So, if he goes can he ever come back?" She lifted her head and he saw a return of her spirit, her bright mind seeking a solution. "Could I buy the portrait once the exhibit is through touring?"

"I don't know. I could check into whether the portrait might be for sale. It wouldn't come cheap."

Kate nodded. "I'll find a way. But could Darach come back after he takes care of things?"

"It's possible. I can't give you the probability. Funny thing about this time travel, other than the continuum of time, there are no rules, no regs, and no guarantees. There is no guarantee Darach can actually get back to 1744. It simply may not happen. Once the portal is identified, it doesn't mean it's an open-door policy."

She reminded him of a Botticelli portrait, radiant and tragic all at once.

"I'm not looking for a guarantee, just a chance."

14

HER WEDDING DAY. Kate drew a deep breath and paused at the arched stone doorway, letting the moment wash over her, through her. Stained glass filtered the sunlight rendering the church's interior dim and cool. Arches, nave and a worn stone floor lent it the feel of old Europe instead of Atlanta. The haunting notes of the bagpipes filled the air.

At the end of the long aisle, Darach waited, resplendent in his kilt. Hamish and Harriett—poor Hamish had finally given in to her standing witness—stood by his side.

Kate smoothed a hand over her dress. The cream silk with fitted sleeves that belled over her wrists was simple and elegant and she'd known the moment she spotted it—it was *the dress*—even without Hamish's seal of approval.

She looked down at the bouquet of cream roses and blue forget-me-nots with one single red velvet rose in the middle. Instead of ribbon, a thin strip of the MacTavish plaid from Darach's kilt knotted the flowers in place.

Was she truly ready to pledge herself to this man who could not stay? Would it be enough to carry only his name and continue to walk alone in life?

The answer welled inside her—a pure joy, a rightness of being. Yes, she, practical, pragmatic Kate Wexford was about to marry a man from another century that she'd only known for a week and a half. She'd never been surer of anything. And for today, for now, she would live in the moment.

She wished, not for the first time, that her mother could have been here—to laugh and join in the whirlwind planning, to stand by Kate's side and share in her joy. She would like Darach, Kate had no doubt. Warm air gusted against the back of her neck, ruffling her hair and then was gone. Kate smiled. Perhaps her mother was here, after all.

She began her walk down the aisle, feeling as if she literally floated down the aisle, buoyed by love and promise and the pipes' sweet melancholy. Darach's eyes met and held hers, silently proclaiming his love. She reached his side and passed her bouquet to Harriett, who was already dabbing at her eyes with a lace hankie.

She and Darach clasped hands. His, warm and big, engulfed hers.

The minister kept it short and sweet. Within minutes they'd promised to love, honor, and cherish one another—Kate had refused a vow of obedience.

"I now pronounce you husband and wife."

Harriett sobbed to beat the band.

"You may kiss your bride."

"Aye. The good part. Give me a kiss, wife."

"Aye. 'Tis my pleasure, husband."

Kate deliberately stepped on his toe.

He framed her face in his hands as if she were precious and fragile. "Wench."

She clasped his wrists in her hands. "Barbarian."

His kiss held tenderness and promise and passion.

"Katie Wexford-MacTavish. Aye, that has a nice ring to it."

KATIE UNLOCKED THE DOOR of the condo and Darach stopped his beautiful bride with a stilling hand. He'd waited a lifetime for her and he wagered they'd do it correctly.

"We will do this right." He swept her up in his arms. "'Tis the groom's duty to carry his bride o'er the threshold."

Her green eyes alight, Kate wound her arms around his neck and nuzzled his chin. "It's also the groom's duty to carry his wife upstairs and fulfill her every need."

He loved her beyond reason. "Must be a strange American custom. Where I'm from that is the wife's duty."

She reached around behind him and closed the door. "Sorry, MacTavish, you're too big for me to carry you upstairs."

He started up to the second floor. "Ah, I can see I'll have to teach you how to be a proper Scots wife."

She flicked her tongue against his neck, which sent a rush of blood straight to his groin. "And it is clear to me you may need a lesson or two in how to be a regular American husband."

He made quick work of the rest of the stairs and entered her bedroom. He bent one knee on her bed and laid her against the pillows and coverlet. "Ah, here is the marital bed, wife." He couldn't seem to say it often enough. Wife. She'd pledged her troth as he had pledged his.

She was stunningly beautiful in her wedding finery but he ached to take it off of her and make her his again. Aye, they'd made love before and it shouldn't be any different this time, but it would be. They'd pledged themselves to each other before God and under the laws of the land and now they'd consummate their vows in the most elemental way between a man and a woman.

He left their banter behind and smoothed her hair

from her face. "Katie-love, I didn't know I could love anyone the way I love you. I didn't know I could feel this way about anyone, the way I feel about you. I care about my people and that is a blend of duty, and obligation and a measure of affection, but 'tis not the same." He drew her hand to his chest, held it against his heart. "I was dead inside. I died that day along with my mother and my brothers. But you resurrected me."

She drew him down to lie by her side. She caressed his cheek, her fingers lingering against his skin. "We've lived parallel lives in different times. I buried myself in my work and kept myself alone, apart. I didn't want to fall in love. You weren't part of my plan. My mother never remarried after my father died. There's a tendency in our family to love deeply and exclusively and there was never any thought that she might find another love. And that's what I've found with you, Darach MacTavish." She smoothed her thumb over his lower lip. "I think it must go along with what Hamish said, sometimes it doesn't matter what we think we want."

He captured her hand in his and pressed a kiss to her delicate blue-veined wrist. "Our souls called to one another and there was naught we could do but heed their cry."

There was nothing more to be said. Words were

unnecessary, superfluous. With no hurried movements, each undressed the other until they lay naked together on their wedding bed.

Darach kissed, touched every silken inch of his wife's skin. She returned his caresses with her hands and mouth. Like a fire stoked to burn through the night, their passion was a steady heat between them.

Lying side by side, facing one another, her leg over his, he entered her. Like two streams converging to form a mighty river, they became one. With each thrust, he gave himself to her, until there was no sense of where he ended and where she began.

THE FOLLOWING AFTERNOON, Darach snapped his book closed with a grunt. Kate, her feet in his lap, put down the medical journal she'd been trying to read except, they were so tuned into one another, her husband's mounting frustration was almost a palpable force in the room.

She swung her feet to the floor, sitting upright on the sofa they shared. "Nothing?"

He put the book on the table and stood. "Nay." He dragged his hands through his black hair. "It's like a huge ocean and I'm but one wave and can do nothing to change the course of the tide."

She picked up a pen and notepad from the round table between the sofa and armchair. "Let's look at your options." She started a list. "You can go to the other leaders and tell them this is what happens on this day. No one will believe you. You can take a page out of a history book with you but I still don't think they'll believe you. That's option one. Option two. You can refuse to fight and you'll be labeled a traitor by your people and you and your people will still endure harsh rule under the British. That still leaves a lot to be desired. Third option, you can fight and you will die at Culloden." The words tasted bitter on her tongue. "If you don't die on the battle-field, the British will find you and kill you. And that's still going to be a bummer for your people." She could make bad jokes or she could burst into tears. Bad jokes seemed her better option. The last thing he needed was a sobbing, clinging wife. "That pretty much sucks worst than the rest."

He nodded, his face grim. "The same options I come up with." He banged his fist on the table, rattling the lamp. "Bluidy hell, I know there is some-thing else out there. I just can't think of it."

"Probably because you're thinking so much *about* it." There had to be an answer. They couldn't just lay down and die on this, literally. They were two reasonably intelligent people and if they put their heads together and kept looking, they had to find an answer. Giving up was not an option.

"Which is why we're going to list every option. We're going to brainstorm. And it doesn't matter how wild or crazy."

"Okay. I've got nothing to add to your list."

"These are options. Not necessarily solutions, but options. Things you could do." She couldn't seem to help herself. She'd sworn she'd never say it, but it came out nonetheless. "You could stay."

The words fell between them. She didn't need to say more. They both knew they could have a good life together. Sweet, hot notes of passion sang between them, punctuated with pleasure's sighs. The contentment of loving and being loved. The giggles of small children.

Darach closed his eyes as if he didn't dare look at the future they could have. "And what becomes of my people, those that have given me their loyalty, their trust?" Pain laced each word. He opened his eyes but didn't look at her.

Desperation drove her to say things she knew she shouldn't. "If you go back you'll die anyway and that won't do them any good. Either way you'd be dead to them."

"And if I stay I would be dead to myself. Ne'er a day passes that I am not tormented by the dream of growing old by your side." His dark eyes reflected that torment. He shook his head, his mouth a tight harsh line. "But I cannae do it and we will not speak of it again. I will either lead my people to safety through this dark time or die trying."

Kate laughed, but she couldn't hide the note of bitterness. "Of all the men in the universe across all time, why did I pick an eighteenth century Highlander with a Moses complex?" Ashamed of her outburst, she pressed her fingertips to her temple. This was not proving to be her finest moment. Darach said nothing and she looked at him in apology. "I'm sorry. I shouldn't have said that. If you weren't the stubborn, complicated man you are, I wouldn't love you so much that I ache."

He smiled at her by way of accepting her apology. "Moses? Mayhap I should grow a beard and proclaim to the English king to let my people go."

Damn him and his gallows humor. "Maybe you should," she said. "I'm sure you'd be devastatingly sexy with a beard. Wait. Since you're going back alone, forget that." She went along with his joke and teased him in return by way of further apology. "I don't need to send you off any sexier than you already are." They both knew she was just talking. She trusted him implicitly. He was one of the most honorable men she'd ever met. Damn, that was part of the problem. His stinking honor. He couldn't just walk away from his people. He was bound to lead them all to their doom.

Maybe…he…should. His eyes met and held hers and she saw an idea working in his eyes. Was it the same idea? "Moses led his people out…" she said.

"…in search of the promised land," he finished the thought. "Just this morning I was reading in one of the library books about Scots who left to seek a new life elsewhere."

Tentative hope clutched at her. "You could emigrate. Would your clan follow you?"

"A fair number. I am sure there would be those who decided to stay, but, aye, a fair number." A broad smile lit his face. He grabbed her wrist and pulled her up from the couch, sending the pen and paper flying. "Katie-love, I think 'tis the key I have been searching for. There is a rightness about this." He caught her up in his arms and swung her about in a circle. His heart beat frantically against her chest.

Elation filled her. She wanted to sing, shout. "I think so too. This feels much more right, even with all the uncertainty, than knowing you die at Drumossie."

"Aye. 'Twas easier to say I did not mind dying when I had nothing to lose." He pressed a hard kiss to her lips. "Even though you will be here, and I will be there, I will carry you with me in my heart."

They were on a roll, she might as well…. "I could come with you."

"No." He set her on her feet with a thud, his hands gripping her arms. "This is your place and your time. You belong here. I've had but a sample of your world and 'tis hard to give it up." He let her go and stepped away from her. "There are too many things you'd sacrifice. Think of the advances in medicine and the things you do to help people every day." He paced to the window, his back to her. "As a woman, you know more freedoms than at any time in the past. 'Tis vastly different to be a woman in 1744. And a woman's lot will not significantly improve any time soon." He turned and faced her. "Were you to go back with me, you'd never know the privileges you know now in your lifetime. And what about this breast cancer that runs in your family? You stand a good chance here, but there'd be nothing for you in my time." His face hardened to resolute implacability. "Absolutely not. We will not speak of it again." He crossed his arms over his chest as if it was the end of the discussion.

This laird of Glenagan having spoken business didn't go over well with her. "But—"

"Think about it, Katie." Dammit, he didn't even give her a chance to talk. "Think about all those things you missed before and you were only there for a day and a night. No electricity. No running water. No telephones. No sleep number beds. No coffee. And what if you are going to have our child? Would you give birth in the middle of a sea voyage with nary a midwife in attendance?"

Damn him. That argument held more sway than all of the others. That argument silenced her.

He shook his head. "Katie-love," his voice softened, quietened, "you no more belong there than I belong here."

15

FOUR DAYS LATER KATE looked out of their hotel room window at their view of Central Park.

"At least it is not raining today," Darach said. He moved in behind, wrapping his arms around her.

Kate bit her lip, trying very very hard to keep herself together. She'd been fine yesterday on the flight from Atlanta to LaGuardia, distracted by Darach's first experience on a plane. Of all the technology he'd encountered, flying seem to captivate him the most.

She'd been fine when they met Hamish for dinner and Darach had laid out his hastily, yet carefully, drawn plans. Hamish had applauded his plan to lead the clan MacTavish to Quebec, which wasn't under British rule, and then to move further west, into un-claimed territory until after the revolutionary war. North America held opportunity, a similar climate and religious freedom.

She'd been fine during their early evening carriage ride through Central Park.

Today, she wasn't so fine. Today it seemed obscene that the sun bathed the city in a radiant light when her heart felt so bleak. And she would keep her bleakness locked inside and not taint the last few hours with the man she loved. She could spend those hours making love to her husband. She'd have a lifetime to mourn after he was gone.

She turned her head and kissed the warm skin of his arm. "Yes, at least it's not raining."

She shifted and slid her arms around his neck. "We've got a couple of hours before we need to meet Hamish at the museum." Three hours to be exact, before he'd meet them at the side door and slip them in ahead of regular hours. Three hours until Darach stepped back in time and she caught a cab for a flight back home and a night shift at the hospital. She fitted her hips to his. "I think just enough time to slip in another lesson on being a proper husband."

He smiled but there was no hiding the melancholy that underscored their banter. "Aye. And I was just thinking you'd have the chance to practice your wifely skills." He backed her up until her legs bumped the mattress.

She fell back and took him down with her. One more time to take him inside her, to know the pleasure, the satisfaction of loving and being loved in not just a carnal but a mystical, spiritual way.

"And I'm thinking this could work out to be mutually beneficial."

THREE HOURS LATER, the streets of New York flashed by the cab window. Darach held Katie's hand. His conscience smote him. He'd done naught to protect her from what she'd need protection from the most—him.

"I'm sorry, Katie-love."

"For what?" Even though a half smile hovered at her mouth, bleakness filled her eyes and he felt pain rolling off her in waves.

Would that he could take her pain and make it his own. But there was naught he could do to assuage her wound. "That all of this happened. It would have been better for you if you had never tumbled through that picture…"

She stopped him with a finger to his lips. "No. Never say that. Never think that." She traced the line of his brow with one finger. "I will never regret the time I've had with you. The price hasn't been too high. I wouldn't give up the time I've had with you, what I've found with you for anything."

She leaned into him, her cheek resting against

his heart, her hair brushing his chin. He breathed in her scent.

"If the picture does not make it back—" he'd tucked a photograph of them on their wedding day into his kilt "—know that I will carry you always in my heart."

The cab pulled over to the curb. Katie took care of the fare and then they both climbed out. She clutched her overnight bag like a lifeline. Darach carried nothing more than he'd come with save their picture held against his chest and the wedding ring on his finger.

They rounded the building to the left, as they'd discussed, and Hamish stood waiting at the side entrance. "Ah, there you are. Come in."

They were all silent as he and Katie followed Hamish. At this point, there was nothing left to say. Their footfalls echoed in the quiet with a hollowness he felt to his core.

Was this what it felt like to walk to the gallows? Surely it could be no grimmer.

They arrived at the portrait. Darach could hardly bear to glance at it. This was where it had begun and this was where it would end.

What had he done? Bound her with vows and a love that would leave her alone and lonely. A decent man would give her leave to get on with her life. "Katie, if you should meet another—"

Her look quelled him. "I won't. Never. I'll bear the MacTavish name with pride."

Aye, he had fallen in love with the finest lass of all time. "If you are…" He glanced toward her flat belly.

"I will." She brought his hands to her lips and kissed them.

She put him from her and he knew instinctively she did so in order not to cling to him. He dared not touch her either, for fear he'd never bear to let her go.

She squared her shoulders. "I love you, Darach MacTavish, laird of Glenagan, chieftain of the clan MacTavish." Her voice rang with pride in who he was.

"Aye, wife. I love you Katie Wexford-MacTavish, healer of men and their souls."

He turned to face the portrait, a man coming face to face with the hangman. Hamish clapped him on the shoulder. "Godspeed."

Kate turned her head the other way as if she couldn't bear watching. With a gentle shove from Hamish, Darach fell into the painting and the vortex of swirling blackness, leaving Katie and her world behind.

"EVENING, DR. WEXFORD." Reddick, the not quite as fresh-faced intern, greeted her that evening. She'd gone straight from the airport to the hospital. She was early for her shift, but she simply couldn't face the emptiness of her condo yet. She wasn't sure whether it was a blessing or a bane that she'd go home to Darach's books and clothes and his lingering presence. She'd finagled the last four days off, no small feat, and now it was time to be back at work and give it one-hundred percent. She returned Reddick's greeting.

"Evening. What's it like tonight?"

"Slow. Quiet."

"Oh." Not what she wanted to hear. She wanted to be so busy she didn't have time to think. She'd had the interminable cab ride and plane trip to think. She knew she'd feel better if she'd cry. She wanted to cry. She wanted to scream and beat her fists against her chest. But she couldn't cry. There was nothing there. She felt as empty and cold inside as one of the cadavers from med school.

She shook her head. This was crazy. She couldn't go through the rest of her life this way. But then she could probably cut herself a little slack. Tomorrow would be better and the day after that and the day after that. It was like a wound. She was still numb from the cauterization, but she'd heal and move forward.

She smiled at Reddick. "Since it's slow, how about I treat you to a double latte?"

Reddick really needed to work on his poker face because his mouth all but dropped open at her offer. He picked his chin up off the floor. "Sure. Thank you, Dr. Wexford."

She'd told Darach she'd bear his name with pride and there was no time like the present. Besides, to talk about him made it seem as if he weren't lost forever to her. "Actually, it's Dr. Wexford-MacTavish. I haven't changed it at the hospital yet, but I got married earlier this week." She smiled at speaking the words aloud, feeling slightly less hollow inside.

Reddick looked very surprised and then he returned her smile. "That's great, Dr. Wexford-MacTavish. Congratulations." There was a pause. "Wexford-MacTavish. That's a bit of a mouthful," Reddick said.

The break room was virtually deserted and Kate fed her money into the machine. She laughed over her shoulder. "It is. But it has a nice ring, don't you think?"

She and Reddick were in mid-toast when Torri entered followed by a couple of lab techs and two nurses. Kate had worked several times with the red-haired nurse, Karen. She was smart, competent and professional—in other words, a pleasure to work with. She'd only seen the lab techs and the other nurse in passing.

Torri eyed the two of them with a catty expression. "Did I miss something?"

Reddick, bless his newbie heart, blurted out. "Dr. Wexford got married. Uh…I mean Dr. Wexford-MacTavish." He flashed a rueful smile Kate's way. "Sorry, it's going to take a while to get used to it."

Torri stopped in her tracks. "MacTavish? The Scottish hunk? He married *you?*"

An image of Darach stretched naked on her bed flashed through her mind. Torri didn't know the half of it. "I suppose Scottish hunk is a fairly accurate description, yes."

Torri's eyes glittered with malice. "Did he need a green card?"

Kate merely smiled when Karen rolled her eyes and mouthed "Bitch" behind Torri's back.

Torri's gaze flew to Kate's left hand, as if she wouldn't believe it until she had visible proof. "That's your ring?"

Kate rubbed her thumb against the band and held out her hand for everyone to see. "Yes. Isn't it beautiful? Blue diamonds set in platinum. Darach commissioned it. It's a one-of-a-kind." She wasn't above rubbing Torri's nose in it.

Everyone seemed to genuinely admire the ring except for the malcontent Dr. Campbell.

"It's certainly different," Torri sniped.

Kate had never understood what made women like Torri tick. Physically, Torri was a beautiful woman. She was smart enough. She made decent money. Why, then, was she such a bitch? Why did she constantly have to denigrate and belittle?

And Torri wasn't through with Kate, yet. "Ladies, you won't believe how yummy he is." She looked Kate over from head to toe, her look clearly saying they'd never believe it because how could he be yummy if he'd chosen Kate. Could she possibly be more insulting? "I can't wait to see him again."

Kate had had enough. She smiled at Torri. "I don't think so. Let's see—exactly how did he describe you?" Kate pretended to ponder for a moment and then snapped her fingers. "Harridan. Yes. That was the exact word he used. Harridan." She nearly laughed at Torri's look of outrage. "You might want to look that up in a dictionary, but it doesn't mean hot." One of the lab techs couldn't stifle a giggle, which earned her a portion of the venomous look Torri had shot toward Kate. Kate shrugged. "Sorry, Torri, he didn't find you quite as yummy as you found him."

Fleeting as it might be, Kate felt infinitely better.

"YOU ARE BACK," Hamish said with a smile of genuine welcome and relief. Of course this was the younger version of Hamish who didn't carry a cell phone and shop incessantly since those things had yet to make their way to his world.

"Aye, I am back." He'd landed in his bedroom, ascertained that his wedding picture had survived the trip, and then had sought out Hamish. He considered it a stroke of luck that he'd encountered no one before finding Hamish on the parapet. The older man appreciated the view from here at the end of a day, despite the cold wind that drove across the moor.

"And not a minute too soon. Everyone is restless, worried that they have lost their laird. There has been much despair amongst them that you had succumbed to your fever."

Just as he'd known, he could never leave his people. They counted on him. Twas his duty to take care of them, to protect them.

"Other than that, has it been quiet?"

"For the most part. Old Ewan had a bit of cattle thieved which we took care of." Hamish's smile said he'd dealt swiftly with those foolish enough to thieve from a MacTavish. "What did you find out?"

Darach filled him in on the bitter history about to unfold in their lives and their country.

A dull red flush of anger tinged Hamish's face.

"The Sassenach outlaw the wearing of the colors and the playing of the pipes?"

"Aye. They consider both signs of war."

Hamish stared out over the moor, as if he could literally see the future advancing. "'Tis dark days indeed on the horizon." He turned his attention to Darach. "But I can see it in your eyes, you have returned with a plan."

Hamish listened attentively as Darach outlined the MacTavish exit strategy.

"It will not be easy," Hamish said when Darach concluded.

Darach squared his shoulders. He looked at the beautiful but merciless moor. He and his people were a rugged lot. The Highlands bred nothing less. "Neither will standing idly by while our way of life and our people die."

"What of the old? They will slow us down."

Darach knew Hamish didn't think they should leave them behind. Hamish tended to see his role as devil's advocate and there would be those in the clan who would ask. "We will naught leave behind anyone who wants to come."

Hamish nodded his satisfaction at Darach's proclamation. "And what might that be?" Hamish asked, pointing to his finger in the waning light.

Despite the seriousness of their subject matter,

Darach couldn't contain his smile. "I got married while I was in the twenty-first century." He pulled out the photograph that had made the journey through time with him, holding the corner tight lest the wind snatch it from him. "Katie makes a bonnie bride, nay?"

Hamish clapped him on the back, a congratulatory grin near splitting his face. "Well, then where is she, man?"

He tucked the picture back into his kilt for safe keeping. "I believe she had to work the night shift. She's a healer at a big hospital," Darach said.

Incredulity replaced his grin. "You married her and she dinnae come back with you? We could use a healer with her skills, especially on the journey we are about to undertake. Do you not remember how she saved the lad before? There was naught we could do for him."

"Aye, I remember. But it changes nothing." The wind had taken on a bitter edge, seeming to cut through to his soul. Darach shook his head. "She does not belong here."

A stubborn cast to his face, Hamish argued with him. "If you are here, how is it she does not belong here?"

"If you do not recall the twenty-first century, then you can't appreciate how much easier life is.

You should see *you* in the twenty-first century. Aye, you are quite fond of the good life." Darach braced himself on the edge of the stone worn smooth by time and the elements. "There are medicines and machines that can save a person's life that we will nae have in our lifetime. And she is not likely to be slaughtered because she is a MacTavish where she is now. Katie is in the safest place for her."

"You know that decision is not totally up to you. Mayhap Katie doesn't want you to keep her safe." The wind increased, howling around them, as if taking up Hamish's cause. "If she decides this is where she wants to be then there is naught you can do to change that."

That's where Hamish was wrong. If Darach could find a way to save his people, he could find a way to save his wife from doing something foolish, too. And he already had an idea…

16

KATE STARED OUT OF HER window at the lights of the city and the Christmas decorations that seemed to be everywhere. One month. Thirty long days and nights since Darach had left. She'd started her period within days of him leaving, so she didn't even have the comfort of his child to hold on to.

As she did often at work and far more often in the quiet loneliness of her condo, she wondered what Darach was doing. How were his plans progressing? Did snow blanket the grounds yet? Was he well? And as usual, her questions remained unanswered.

How ironic. To an observer, there was no visible sign that her life had changed. Things were just as they had been. She went to work. She came home. No one could tell she'd changed forever, irrevocably. She'd told herself time would help. How much time would it take? She still felt as cold and empty as she had that day in New York when Darach had heeded his call to duty and forsaken her world for his.

She leaned her head against the cool glass and closed her eyes. When would it change? When would it get better?

Never.

Like a brilliant flash of light in the darkest hour, she realized with brutal insight that she'd lied to Darach. She'd told him the price of what they'd found together wasn't too high.

Yet, here she sat in her comfortable condo, alone, because his obligations would never free him to be here with her and she was too cowardly to walk away from all her comfortable life offered.

What, other than a few logistical details, was to keep her from going back to New York and walking through that portrait, back in time and back to the man who meant more to her than any of this ever could?

Whoa, sister. She'd had just a taste of the past and hadn't particularly liked it. How would she fare with a steady diet of no technology and roughing it for the rest of her life?

But then again, would she enjoy living this way indefinitely? This wasn't living, this was existing. She'd had a taste of living and that's what she wanted, even if it was a couple of centuries ago.

She pushed away from the window, feeling more alive than she'd felt since Darach had left. She had plans to make, details to see to, for she was about to take a journey of a lifetime, for a lifetime.

DARACH STARED INTO the fire in his room and tried to put the thought of visiting Katie from his mind, but the idea refused to quiet. Preparations for their journey were coming along nicely. Nonetheless he could not, would not go forward to see Katie. What if he got there and couldn't come back? What if he got there and couldn't force himself to return to the people who counted on him?

Every day he thought of her, longed for her. Every day he fought this battle with himself. How long before he lost the battle and his self-respect? And what of Hamish's prediction that Katie would come to him? Would he have the strength to send her back? Could he bear to let her go yet again?

Resolute, Darach turned back from the fire that had held no answers and faced the portrait. The answer lay within his heart. He knew what he had to do.

KATE PAID THE CAB DRIVER, stepped out onto the New York City sidewalk, and stood before the museum housing the Sex Through the Ages exhibit.

What a difference since she'd stood in this same

spot nearly two months before. Christmas had come and gone and she'd celebrated the season and her impending new life. She'd been incredibly busy wrapping up the details of this life and preparing for the next. And now it was all done and there was no more hectic activity to occupy her. She felt a heady, almost giddy sense of freedom. She didn't allow even a smidgeon of trepidation.

A pedestrian jostled past her and she wrapped her coat more tightly about her and walked up to the museum door. She purchased a ticket and didn't bother to tell the woman who pointed her in the direction of the exhibit that she well remembered it from before.

Early afternoon had brought few museum visitors and Kate wandered about by herself, searching for Hamish. She could've called him on his cell, but she'd wanted to simply show up, a fait accompli. Her heels clicked on the hard-surface floor, heralding her arrival. He looked up about the time she spotted him near the historical dildo display.

His smile offered a genuine welcome. "Kate. What a surprise." He hugged her. "You're looking well. A bit thinner perhaps."

All the years she'd longed to drop ten pounds, who'd ever known it was as simple as having no appetite because you missed someone so desperately? But that was about to change.

She returned his hug and dropped her arms to her side. "Thank you. You're looking very well yourself."

His smile faded and he took her hands in his. "Kate, I need to tell you…"

"Wait. I have some exciting news. I resigned from my job, sold all my possessions and I have two bags packed in the hopes they can make the trip with me. That's why I'm here. I want to go back, Hamish. I'd rather live in the 1700s with Darach than the twenty-first century without him."

Hamish winced, looking decidedly agitated, and gripped her hands tighter. "You can't go back, Kate."

She disengaged her hands. She knew he wasn't doing it on purpose, but Hamish was hurting her. "I know Darach didn't think it was a good idea." She smiled when she imagined the look on his face. "In fact, I'm pretty sure he's not going to be happy with me but he'll get used to the idea. He'll have to." She crossed her arms over her chest, the way her stubborn husband usually did. "Because I'm going."

Hamish shook his grey head, pity shining in his blue eyes. "No. You don't understand what I'm telling you. You can't go back, Kate, because you have no way to get there. The painting was destroyed." Her stomach dropped. What? He had to be mistaken. "We're still trying to figure out what happened. It seems to have been a freak accident. Nothing else in the exhibit was damaged."

Kate sank to the bench in the middle of the room, not sure her legs could continue to support her. No longer sure of anything. "Destroyed? How could that be? How is it possible nothing else was harmed?"

Hamish sat on the cushioned bench beside her and wrapped a comforting arm about her shoulders. "I think something happened to it on Darach's end. Either Glenagan was overrun or something happened and the painting was destroyed…"

He paused and she sensed his reluctance. "Or?" Her voice came through as little more than a hoarse whisper.

"Or Darach destroyed it himself. Either way, neither of you can get to the other, because your portal is gone."

No! Kate swallowed the primal scream that resonated though her head. She felt as if Hamish had kicked her in the gut, expelling all the breath from her body, replacing all the air with water. The tears that had refused to come before welled up and spilled forth.

HAMISH HAD HANDLED several different situations over the centuries as he'd floated through the universe. The one thing he really, really couldn't handle was a crying woman. All his knowledge flew out the proverbial window and he simply felt helpless. And Kate wasn't just crying, she was mourning as if her heart had been ripped from her body.

He patted ineffectually at her shoulder. "There, there. If you'll just stop crying…don't cry now…if you can stop…that's it, don't cry…we'll see if we can't think of something."

"What can we do?" She mopped her face with the back of her hand and sat up straighter. "I'll do whatever I need to do. Just tell me what to do."

No more tears was a good place to start. "I'm not sure what to do yet, but don't start crying again. We'll put our heads together."

She narrowed her eyes and he could all but see the wheels turning in her head. "I'm sure all the items in the collection are insured and cataloged. Is there a photo of the portrait?"

"Yes."

She stood and paced to the wall and back, shoulders back, head up, resolute. "Then we'll find an artist to recreate it. We'll have an artist copy it."

How to tell the lass the next bit of news? "I'm not sure that having another artist paint it will give it the same portal properties."

"It's worth a try."

"Well, I think I may have someone for you." Could he still do it? Would he have lost his touch? After all, it had been nearly three centuries.

"Great. I want the best. Money's no object."

He'd be glad to help…if there was any help to be had. "There's no fee involved."

"How can that be—" she whirled to face him, comprehension dawning "—wait…you. It's you, isn't it? You were the artist." Accusation shone in her eyes. "I asked and you said the artist was unknown."

He nodded. "I painted it over two-hundred sixty-five years ago. I could hardly tell you then that I was the artist and later…well, it seemed gratuitous to bring it up. I'm not sure if I can do it now. And even if I did there's no guarantee that it will work the same way. You have to understand that."

"I understand." She nodded. Ready to move on to the next matter of business. "How long do you think it will take? How soon can you start?"

"I'll need supplies—"

She interrupted. "Make a list. I can have them ready today."

"Okay. So that means I can start tomorrow. Two weeks. Tops. Maybe less."

"Tell me where to have them delivered and they'll be waiting for you."

He scribbled out a supply list and his address on a piece of paper and handed it to her.

"This should get me started." God knows he didn't want her to start crying again, but she needed to think this through. "On the outside chance, and it is an outside chance, that this painting serves as a portal, what will you do if you get there and Darach is gone? If the portrait was destroyed, there's a good chance Darach could be dead. And I could very well be dead too. What will you do then?"

"First, I don't believe he's gone. He and I have such a strong connection, I know I would feel it if he was dead." She seemed so sure, so confident, he wanted to believe it as well. "But, if he is then I'll carry on the MacTavish legacy as best I can. This is the thing—my life here is over. I've felt dead inside since Darach left and I finally realized why. I was dead inside because I no longer have a life here. My life is with Darach."

He'd yet to meet two people that belonged together more. "I'll try my best for you, Kate."

Her eyes held his. "It has to work."

He hoped for her sake it did.

"EVERYTHING IS RUNNING according to plan. We're right where we should be according to my time line," Darach said to Hamish at the end of yet another day. Each seemed to now run headlong into another.

"Aye. We will get through the winter and with the coming of spring, we should be on our way to a new life." Hamish shifted from foot to foot, a sure sign he had a question he wanted to ask but was hesitant about doing so.

"What is it man? Speak up." Darach knew his tone rang sharp but he was soul weary. His days were long but the empty nights were longer still.

Hamish gestured toward the empty spot on the wall. "What happened to the portrait?"

"I broke it into pieces and I burned it." It had been akin to gutting himself with his own dagger.

Hamish paled. "But…now Kate cannae come to you or you to her."

He knew a grim satisfaction. "Exactly."

"But what if all was not as it should be?"

Was Hamish yet once again playing devil's advocate or did he know something? It mattered naught. "Then 'tis time for it to be. Katie belongs in her world and I belong in mine. Ne'er the twain shall meet again."

Hamish wrung his hands. "I am not so sure you did the right thing. Not so sure at all."

"You don't have to be. I am." He was laird of

Glenagan and no one need second guess his decision, not even Hamish. "When you go down, send up Coira."

"For what?" For the second time in as many seconds, Hamish questioned him.

"What do you think, man? She is a comely wench."

Hamish looked horrified. "You do not mean to tumble her?"

He ignored the sick feeling in his gut. "Aye. I've said it before and I'll say it again. When it comes to a tumble, one lass is as good as another." This pining for Katie was driving him mad. He'd thought destroying the painting would staunch the endless need for her that coursed through him like a burn tumbling swift and cold through the landscape of his heart. He'd pledged her his troth. Now, surely if he broke that vow it would release him from this ravening hunger, this need.

"You don't want to do this, Darach," Hamish said.

"I think you forget yourself. Leave and send me Coira."

Hamish left without saying another word, anger and disapproval marking his stride from the room.

Darach tried to put the images of Katie from his mind. Her standing before the fire in this room, her lying on his bed, the wash of moonlight over her cheek, the sound of her laughter, the echo of her moan as she came beneath him. Her memories plagued him like demons, driving him mad. It mattered not that Hamish neither understood nor approved. Darach needed to banish those memories and Coira seemed just the way to do it.

Within a few minutes a knock sounded. He crossed the room and opened the door. A comely lass with flaxen hair and a generous bosom stood on the other side. Her skin was not quite so fine as Katie's and her hair wasn't shorn short in the manner of Katie's, but in the shadows, away from the fire's light, she could pass for the other woman.

"Hamish sent me, my laird."

The voice was definitely different. It definitely wasn't the sweet melody of Katie's voice. "Aye, at my order. Enter, Coira."

Coira's husband, much older than she, had died last year. Coira, being a widow, was said to be up for a bit of sport.

"If you have a need my laird, I am here to serve you." She boldly stepped forward and ran her hand down his chest. Her touch did nothing to warm him.

"Mayhap I've a need or two you could help me with," he said, shifting her out of the firelight. She smelled of peat fire, which wasn't unpleasant, but it didn't tease his senses and arouse him the way Katie's scent did.

Coira smiled and without further ado tugged her shift over her head. She stood before him, all ripe curves beneath her thin chemise.

The devil curse him. He couldn't do this. What was he thinking? He could tumble every lass from here to Glasgow and it would do nothing to erase Katie from his heart and his mind. 'Twould only blacken his soul.

"Put your clothes back on, lass. 'Tis not that kind of need I have." Better that she be a bit embarrassed than have the whole clan think him daft, which was, at this point, a distinct possibility. "I have a need of another shirt. I understand you are clever with a needle."

Coira tugged her dress back on, her face flushed red. "Aye. Forgive my boldness. I misunderstood."

"Nay. 'Twas my original intent. But I find that my heart belongs to another and 'twould not be fair to any of us to put you in that position."

Far from being angry, Coira beamed in near adoration. "That is so romantic. You are a man of honor and I am honored you would think of tumblin' me. She is a lucky lass."

That struck him as a bit of convoluted female logic. Mayhap Coira, though comely, was simple of mind.

"Nay, I am a lucky man."

He was two-hundred sixty-two years behind her and destined for a life of celibacy because his wife had ruined him for any other woman.

17

"TA DA." HAMISH PULLED the cloth off and revealed the painting beneath it.

"Other than the fact that it isn't aged like the previous one and it's acrylics rather than oils, it looks the same to me," Kate said. The same longing she'd always experienced, the same frisson of anticipation, the same scent from Darach, all assailed her. She felt alive, gloriously happily alive once again. "And it feels the same."

Kate pulled her two suitcases, trunks ready, forward. "So, let's give it a go."

"You're sure you're ready?"

"I've been ready for a week." She smiled, barely checking her excitement. "And you know it, since I've been breathing down your neck the entire time."

She'd spent the last week having facials, pedicure, manicure, and a sea algae body wrap. She wanted to look as good as possible when she got there because she fully anticipated MacTavish was going to be madder than hell when she showed up, especially if he had, in fact, destroyed the painting to keep her in her century. And she had a feeling that was precisely the case. Her husband wasn't a man of half-measures and he'd told her to stay.

"Do I want to know what you've got in the cases?"

Other than breathing down his neck to finish, she and Hamish had had minimal contact. She'd wanted every second of his attention and spare time focused on re-creating the portrait as soon as possible. "You should, so that you know what to do with them in case they don't go with me. Gold and jewelry in this one, which is why it weighs so much. I converted as much of my money as I could to gold and also bought up as much fine jewelry as possible." She grinned. "My contribution to the clan's migration. This case is full of antibiotics, six month birth control shots, and a couple of medical resource books. I slipped in a pair of silk pajamas, but other than that…when in Rome, do as the Romans do." She tugged at her dress beneath her heavy woolen cloak. "Are you sure this looks okay on me? Does it make me look fat?"

"You look lovely. Just like an eighteenth century chieftain's wife should look. They did a marvelous job."

She wanted to go back, desperately, and she'd take the trip any way she could get it but she was praying like hell she didn't show up naked this time. She'd contacted a costume designer before she left Atlanta and had told the woman she was participating in a period history drama. The woman had come up with a complete, historically accurate wardrobe for her. But she still thought she looked kind of hippy in the dresses. Oh, well, if she looked fat in it, hopefully all the other women in the clan looked equally heavy.

"Thank you for everything." She hugged him. "I don't expect to see you again in this lifetime. But keep an eye out for a MacTavish. I'll be sending them to find you."

Was that a tear in his eye? "It will be a pleasure to meet your and Darach's progeny."

"And if no one shows up by next week, you know what to do?"

"Yes. The money's in a Swiss bank account and if no MacTavish comes forward with your letter to claim it, then the money's to anonymously go to fund international medical relief work."

She patted the letter on her hip. It would be given to her and Darach's children and passed through generations until two-hundred-and-sixty-two years elapsed and brought them to today. Hopefully a MacTavish, with letter in hand, would arrive to claim the inheritance she'd left in a Swiss bank account. Since no time would elapse in the present world, Hamish would see her children's children's children's children here before she'd ever had a chance to conceive in real time. Freaky thought to wrap her head around, but she liked the idea of being an eccentric, long-dead benefactress.

"It's time, Hamish. I'm ready."

She shrugged into her backpack that was much like the carry-on piece you used when you traveled by plane. The one bag that was essential in case they lost your luggage in-flight. She grabbed the handle of each monstrously large case in each hand. Hamish took her arm and gave her a gentle shove.

Much as before, she was spinning, whirling in darkness, the air rushing past her at dizzying speeds. And much as before, she opened her eyes and found herself on Darach's bed. She double-checked. Woohoo! She wasn't naked this time.

Damn. The bags hadn't made it.

Thunk.

Thunk.

They landed on either side of the bed. Must've been the weight factor that accounted for the time delay.

"What the bluidy hell?" Darach turned from where he'd stood facing the fire.

He was beautiful. The most beautiful sight she'd ever seen...and boiling angry to boot.

"Hi." She offered a small wave. "I was just in the neighborhood and thought I'd drop in."

DARACH STOOD FROZEN, drinking in the sight of Katie, his Katie, on his bed. He wasn't sure whether he wanted to kiss her endlessly or strangle her. He settled for something in between.

"What the bluidy hell are you doing here?"

Katie smiled but her green eyes held a wariness—as well they should. "Now, honey..."

"Do not try your honeyed tongue on me, you bluidy hard-headed wench." He couldn't believe she'd defied him. How could he protect her if she didn't let him? "I told you to stay home."

Her eyes flashed and she jumped up from the bed. "Me, hard-headed?" She closed the gap between them. God's tooth but she smelled good. She'd lost that conciliatory tone and stormed over to him. Next she'd be poking his bluidy chest. "How about you try that on for size? And I couldn't stay home until I got home, you big barbarian Scot. This is my home. Not Glenagan, but where you are." *Poke.* "And the more I thought about it...well, good husbands are hard to find and you were coming along so nicely in the training, how could I just let you go? I'd invested too much time and energy in your training to have to start all over again."

Aye, but she was a beauty, his wife. Another thought occurred to him. "Are you with bairn?"

"No. And I think we should wait until we get to Quebec. I'm thinking seasickness is bad enough without adding morning sickness to it."

"How did you get here?" He looked at the blank spot on the wall.

"Ah, so you did destroy the painting?" *Poke*.

She had some nerve getting her ire up. "I just want to protect you. Your world is so much safer than this one, Katie-love."

"I didn't have a life without you there—I had an existence." Her tone softened and took on the nuance of a caress, sliding over him like warm honey. "I don't need your protection. I just need your love. Don't you understand, you daft Scot?"

Instead of another poke, she slid her hand over his chest. His body tingled all over. For the first time since he'd traveled back through the portrait and left her behind he felt alive. He kept his hands by his side. If he touched her, held her, he wasn't sure he could ever let her go.

"Aye. I do understand. That's what it's been like for me as well. But how did you come?"

"Hamish repainted the portrait." God's tooth, the lass was even comely when she smirked.

And as alive as he felt, there was naught to do but send her back to a safer place and time. "Aye. Then there is naught to stop me from having him repaint it on this end and send you back."

"Don't even try it, big boy." She linked her arms about his neck, a satisfied smile curving her mouth. "It won't work."

"It has worked before," he countered. He grasped her arms, trying to unfasten them from about his neck but she stayed fast like a stubborn exotic orchid determined to bloom on the wind-swept moor.

"It's worked before because need was the key. We needed one another. Now we have one another. There is no need on the other end to pull me back in time. It's a very nice portrait of you and I wouldn't mind looking at it for the rest of my life, so if you really want him to re-create it, go ahead, although I think it's going to be rather cumbersome to transport. But it's not going to make any difference as to whether I stay or go. I'm here. You're stuck with me." For good measure she jumped up and wrapped her legs around his waist with a cheeky grin.

He damn near toppled over at her surprise

attack. With blinding insight, he realized Hamish had been proven right. Sometimes it mattered not what he wanted.

He caught her buttocks in his hands and the fiery heat he knew with Katie scorched through him. "What am I going to do with you Katie-love?"

"I have an idea or two I'm willing to share with you." She scattered kisses along his jaw. "You could start by tying me to the bed again."

A sense of rightness washed over him. "'Tis a nice dress you're wearing, but I preferred when you showed up naked."

She smiled up at him, her green eyes brimming with mischief and love. "I can definitely help you with that, Highlander."

Epilogue

HAMISH MADE ONE last round. Tonight the exhibit closed in New York. Next stop, Chicago.

Footsteps echoed on the museum's wood floor. He looked up. A couple approached.

The woman was dark. The man, by contrast, fair. Hamish had never laid eyes on either before, but a vague sense of the familiar echoed through him.

The woman hailed him from a distance. "Excuse me, sir. We're looking for Hamish."

A knowing, a moment of recognition danced down his spine. "Then you're in luck, Miss. I'm Hamish. And who might you be?"

The woman stood tall and slender, her straight short hair as black as a raven's wing, her green eyes piercing. The man, his flaxen curls brushing his broad shoulders, regarded him with eyes as dark and fathomless as a starless night. The man stepped forward. "I'm Gavin MacTavish and this is my sister, Isobel. I hope you don't think us odd, but we have a letter that's been in our family and passed down for two-hundred-and-sixty-two years. It Instructs us to meet you here this evening." He pulled a folded letter, ragged and weary with age, from his pocket.

Hamish's heart soared. Yes, but of course. Kate and Darach's offspring—it would be what, six, seven generations? But it was there in Gavin's breadth of shoulder and tall stature, the directness of his dark gaze. And the woman with her fearless approach and green eyes could be none other than Kate and Darach's progeny. Isobel and Gavin. Darach's mother's and brother's names, passed down through generations.

He smiled at the siblings. "No. I don't think you're odd at all. I've been hoping to meet you." He ushered them toward the door. "The museum is closing, but there's a coffee shop around the corner. I can explain the letter and I'd like to hear all about your family."

The two shared a cautious look. Isobel gave an almost imperceptible nod.

This time it was she who spoke for the two of them. "We'd be glad to join you for a coffee. But exactly who are you?"

Hamish smiled, feeling very much at ease with the man and woman who reminded him so much of Kate and Darach.

"I'm a very old friend of the family."

Stability is highly overrated....

Dana Logan's world had always revolved around her children. Now they're all grown up and don't seem to need anything she's able to give them. Struggling to find her new identity, Dana realizes that it's about time for her to get "off her rocker" and begin a new life!

Off Her Rocker

by Jennifer Archer

Available August 2006
TheNextNovel.com

HN53

Page-turning drama...

Exotic, glamorous locations...

Intense emotion and passionate seduction...

Sheikhs, princes and billionaire tycoons...

This summer, may we suggest:

THE SHEIKH'S DISOBEDIENT BRIDE
by Jane Porter

On sale June.

AT THE GREEK TYCOON'S BIDDING
by Cathy Williams

On sale July.

THE ITALIAN MILLIONAIRE'S VIRGIN WIFE

On sale August.

With new titles to choose from every month,
discover a world of romance in our books written
by internationally bestselling authors.

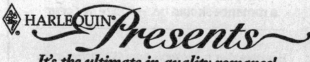

**Hidden in the secrets of antiquity,
lies the unimagined truth...**

Introducing

ROGUE
ANGEL™

a brand-new line filled with mystery
and suspense, action and adventure,
and a fascinating look into history.

And it all begins with DESTINY.

In a sealed crypt in
France, where the
terrifying legend of
the beast of Gevaudan
begins to unravel,
Annja Creed discovers
a stunning artifact
that will seal her destiny.

*Available every other
month starting
July 2006, wherever
you buy books.*

GRA1

If you enjoyed what you just read,
then we've got an offer you can't resist!

Take 2 bestselling love stories FREE!

Plus get a FREE surprise gift!

Clip this page and mail it to Harlequin Reader Service®

IN U.S.A.	IN CANADA
3010 Walden Ave.	P.O. Box 609
P.O. Box 1867	Fort Erie, Ontario
Buffalo, N.Y. 14240-1867	L2A 5X3

YES! Please send me 2 free Harlequin® Blaze™ novels and my free surprise gift. After receiving them, if I don't wish to receive anymore, I can return the shipping statement marked cancel. If I don't cancel, I will receive 6 brand-new novels each month, before they're available in stores! In the U.S.A., bill me at the bargain price of $3.99 plus 25¢ shipping and handling per book and applicable sales tax, if any*. In Canada, bill me at the bargain price of $4.47 plus 25¢ shipping and handling per book and applicable taxes**. That's the complete price and a savings of at least 10% off the cover prices—what a great deal! I understand that accepting the 2 free books and gift places me under no obligation ever to buy any books. I can always return a shipment and cancel at any time. Even if I never buy another book from Harlequin, the 2 free books and gift are mine to keep forever.

151 HDN D7ZZ
351 HDN D72D

Name	(PLEASE PRINT)	
Address	Apt.#	
City	State/Prov.	Zip/Postal Code

Not valid to current Harlequin® Blaze™ subscribers.

Want to try two free books from another series?
Call 1-800-873-8635 or visit www.morefreebooks.com.

* Terms and prices subject to change without notice. Sales tax applicable in N.Y.
** Canadian residents will be charged applicable provincial taxes and GST.
All orders subject to approval. Offer limited to one per household.
® and ™ are registered trademarks owned and used by the trademark owner and/or its licensee.

BLZ05   ©2005 Harlequin Enterprises Limited.

HARLEQUIN Romance

A family saga begins to unravel
when the doors to the Bella Lucia
Restaurant Empire are opened...

The Brides of Bella Lucia

A family torn apart by secrets,
reunited by marriage

AUGUST 2006

Meet Rachel Valentine, in
HAVING THE FRENCHMAN'S BABY
by Rebecca Winters

Find out what happens when a night of passion is followed
by a shocking revelation and an unexpected pregnancy!

SEPTEMBER 2006

The Valentine family saga continues with
THE REBEL PRINCE by Raye Morgan

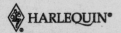

HARLEQUIN®

American ROMANCE®

IS PROUD TO PRESENT A GUEST APPEARANCE BY

QUILL
BOOK
AWARD
WINNING
AUTHOR

NEW YORK TIMES bestselling author

DEBBIE MACOMBER

The Wyoming Kid

The story of an ex–rodeo cowboy,
a schoolteacher and their journey to the altar.

"Best-selling Macomber, with more than
100 romances and women's fiction titles
to her credit, sure has a way of pleasing readers."
—*Booklist* on *Between Friends*

**The Wyoming Kid is available from
Harlequin American Romance in July 2006.**